'You're a lou

He openly laughe
I was thinking yo
leaving you alone!'

'I am!' Jane snapped. 'But I don't like being mixed up in your little games.'

'What little games?' Miguel queried.

'As if you didn't know!' she sneered.

He blew her a kiss. 'I'm not sure I like being reminded that I am sometimes a bad boy...'

Dear Reader

A new year is starting and now is the time to think about the kind of stories you've enjoyed reading during the past year and the stories you would like to read throughout this coming year. As Valentine's Day approaches, why not dream up the most perfect romantic evening for yourself? No doubt it will include a sprinkling of charm, a good degree of atmosphere, a healthy amount of passion and love, and of course your favourite Mills & Boon novel. Keep romance close to your heart—make this year special!

The Editor

A born romantic, **Kristy McCallum** is lively, fun-loving and happily married to a very good-looking man. She has three children, three cats, one dog and other animals she adores. She lives in a particularly beautiful part of the West Country but it rains quite often, so travel to the sun features prominently in her plans. She hopes her readers share her belief that that special man should be kind, amusing and sexy, and passionately in love with her.

Recent titles by the same author:

TIGER MOON

SOMETHING WORTH FIGHTING FOR

BY

KRISTY McCALLUM

MILLS & BOON LIMITED
ETON HOUSE   18-24 PARADISE ROAD
RICHMOND   SURREY   TW9 1SR

*First published in Great Britain 1992
by Mills & Boon Limited*

© Kristy McCallum 1992

*Australian copyright 1992
Philippine copyright 1993
This edition 1993*

ISBN 0 263 77908 4

*Set in Times Roman 11 on 12 pt.
01-9302-47588 C*

Made and printed in Great Britain

CHAPTER ONE

THE intense blue of the sea, today with only the smallest of waves to disturb its sapphire serenity, filled Jane with exhilaration as she balanced more confidently on the white board beneath her feet. There was just enough wind to fill the brightly coloured sail that she still held with the slightly over-firm grip of the beginner as she began to tack her way out of the small bay towards the shimmering brightness of the open Mediterranean.

She'd cracked it! At long last, after a week of feeling more and more like a half-drowned rat, she'd actually learned to windsurf! No more lessons from Hans; she was free now to enjoy herself in her own time, confident in her ability to handle this sport, if not as an expert then at least with enough ability for her own enjoyment.

She knew she looked good silhouetted against the brightness that surrounded her, her short dark hair smooth and sleek against her head, a legacy of her swim. Fine-boned and fragile-looking, she was in reality quite tough, but men never believed it. They'd been trying to take care of her ever since her early teens, but she'd had enough of being told all the time what she couldn't do.

'Jane, you aren't strong enough to handle the sail out of the bay,' Hans had told her, and that had made her mad!

'Françoise, that French girl, took the board out yesterday and you never said a word!' she complained. 'Anyway, she's the same size as I am, so where's the difference?'

Hans had laughed at her. 'She's been windsurfing for years, and before that she sailed. She understands the winds, and you don't, not yet...'

'But there's hardly any wind today!' she protested. 'It isn't even worth my while to hire one of your boards unless I go out of the bay.'

Hans looked at her shrewdly, one hand stroking his fine luxuriant moustache. 'If you really want to leave the shelter of the bay, so...' he shrugged his shoulders '...I can't stop you. But you'd do better to wait, all the same. Why don't you take out the small sail just to try it at first?'

Jane was indignant. 'You mean the sail you use to teach the children?' She was fairly sure that now his hand was covering his mouth to hide a smile.

'Why not?' She didn't feel any better at the sight of his now open amusement, but discretion had her masking her own feelings at this point.

'It'll take me ages to tack out of the bay with that, because there isn't enough wind!' she complained, but he'd had enough of her and just shrugged, his attention already turning towards another potential customer.

Jane pretended to give in, dropping her eyes in submission, but a fierce determination was building inside her. She took her usual board and sail, but she was going to show them all that although she was small she was tough! She'd sail out of the bay and make Hans eat his words if it was the last thing she'd do!

Halfway across the bay she misjudged the path of an incoming speedboat and was forced to drop her sail as it swept past her. As she tried to keep her balance, when the board rocked violently in its wake, the boat came round again in a tight circle before throttling back to come in really close. The churning wake was too much for her this time, and she fell in. Furious, she hauled herself out, prepared to give whoever it was a piece of her mind. She shook the water out of her face, sat up on the board and prepared to do battle.

'What a surprise! I thought you'd given up holidays on Mallorca for good.' That amused, faintly accented voice could only belong to one man.

'Miguel!' She blinked the last of the water out of her eyes, and forgot the last five years, caught once more in the web of the most charismatic man she'd ever met. She shook her head, trying to clear the mist. Come on, girl! she told herself. You're twenty-two, not seventeen . . .

'None other! Do you know, I had the impression that you've been avoiding us? Don't tell me you've had a change of heart?' His wicked black eyes were considering her body with such dedicated attention that she couldn't stop a blush spreading like a forest fire over her face.

Furious at the way her emotions were letting her down when she needed all her cool, she snapped back at him, 'You're absolutely right! I'm on the island only——' she heavily emphasised that last word '—because I've got a summer job.' It was impossible to ignore the exceedingly decorative blonde sitting next to him, who looked quite at home and relaxed about the unscheduled stop, and Jane felt instantly inadequate compared to such cool, elegant beauty. 'Don't let me keep you!' she finished, hoping and praying that he'd leave her alone.

'You're not intending to leave the bay on that windsurfer, are you?' he queried. She might have guessed that he was still bossy and interfering as far as she was concerned.

'And if I am it's nothing to do with you!' she shouted back, instantly losing her temper with him just as she used to when she was a teenager.

'Don't be silly, Jane! The wind's too strong out of the bay for you to manage the sail. Surely you're not still so childish that you can't accept well-meaning advice?'

What was she going to do when it was put like that? She might feel like choking him, but women in their twenties controlled themselves, so perhaps it was better to pretend to submit. 'OK, I'll stay in the bay! It was nice seeing you again...' Without wasting any more time she was up on her feet and praying that her new-found skills wouldn't let her down. She pulled the sail up with commendable aplomb, and with a casual wave of her hand was on her way.

It was maddening to be confined until Miguel should leave the bay, but she had no alternative. As she tacked her way slowly towards the headland, always looking for more wind, her thoughts were full of the tormentor of her youth. He hadn't changed, and she gritted her teeth in frustration at the thought that he was around, and that he would tell his sister she was on the island. Why should he have had to come into this bay and seen her? Come to that, what was he doing on the island at all? Mind you, he'd always had eyes like a cat's, never missing a trick, and she supposed that even he was entitled to an occasional holiday, particularly when his family owned the most beautiful villa not all that far away. Still, it was bad luck that once more his image should be imprinted so violently on to her consciousness. He was still the most charismatic man she'd ever met, even though she'd spent the last five years denying it to herself.

Later she heard his boat coming up close behind her, and braced herself against the wake as once more he circled her, but it was only a token tease this time as he headed out to sea with his blonde companion. As her board rocked, Jane was reciting to herself all the rude names she knew, but his interference was all she needed to bolster up her courage.

She'd show him! Miguel de Tarrago had always been far too fond of having his own way, and it didn't look as if he'd changed in the slightest since she'd last seen him.

As she left the shelter of the bay, the wind strengthened surprisingly, putting a strain on her arms, and she strove to keep her balance as the board seemed to leap forward with the eagerness of a greyhound let out of its trap. She was moving through the water faster than she would have thought possible a few short minutes ago.

Part of her was exhilarated by the speed, but underneath she was a little frightened. The wind was ten times more powerful than anything she was used to in the shelter of the bay. Had she bitten off more than she could chew in her eagerness to prove herself? Already she was far further out to sea than she had intended to venture, and every minute the waves got choppier, making it more and more difficult to balance.

A sudden change in the direction of the wind settled matters. With a total loss of dignity Jane once more fell with surprising force into the blue waters. She came up gasping for air and simply furious with herself, but she was to discover that away from the shelter of the bay she found it virtually impossible to get going again. She just did not have the strength to cope with the sail against the much stiffer sea breeze.

Pride ensured that she was in a fair way to exhausting herself before she was prepared to give in. After half an hour of repeated duckings she was reduced to sitting forlornly on the board. It was only then she realised how much stronger the wind had got, and how much she had drifted away from the bay where she had started. Hans must have seen her take the board out, and he must be just punishing her a little for her silliness; that was why she couldn't see his small boat coming to her rescue.

She began to get really frightened as the waves got bigger and bigger and it was only on their crests that she could still see land. What was going to happen to her, and, more importantly, her job? She was out here all summer as cook to one of the exclusive villas that surrounded the bay.

It was her first proper job and she was supposed to be preparing dinner for twelve this evening, not lost at sea. A wave of cold panic swept over her. Her boss, Lady Waters, was kind and easygoing up to a point, but she wouldn't be best pleased if her first dinner party of the summer went wrong. Thank God she'd already made the gazpacho this morning, and prepared the main course. Even so, there was still quite a lot to be done which even Kate, the girl who came in to help in the evening, wouldn't be able to cope with alone.

Jane gave a small moan. Who knew she'd taken out the board? No one from her villa; they were all resting after eating one of her delicious cold lunches. Even if someone had seen her go down, would they be able to find her now the seas were so big? She'd always heard the Mediterranean was a treacherous sea, but not even she could have believed how quickly it had changed.

It was more than a bit shaming to discover that she was calling for Miguel; willing him to come out in his boat to find her. Why, he ought to know that she'd be almost certain to do the opposite of what he told her! So why wasn't he out here looking for her? Because he's probably making love to that blonde! an inner voice told her. And you've never been important to him, just his sister's little friend, whom he liked to boss around and tease.

With difficulty she stifled a small sob and gave herself a stern talking-to. She wasn't in any danger of drowning, and with luck she would be drifting in to the next big bay with its port. There were always so many boats going in and out, one of them must see her. Apprehensively her big grey eyes tried to check her immediate surroundings, but because she was so low in the water it was impossible for her to see very far, or more important, be seen.

She became increasingly desperate when no one appeared to be aware of her, although she saw a number of boats returning to the port. Her desperation began to be fuelled by the very beauty of her surroundings. The wind might be blowing, and the waves were beginning to have white horses, but the sky was still blue, and the heaving waters were still a deep sapphire colour.

Hopeless tears were running down her face, mixed with salty spray from the sea, when she heard the powerful note of a boat's engine. It didn't sound like Miguel's, but she was by now past caring. She risked falling in again by standing up unsteadily to wave both hands, before once more she was forced down into a kneeling position and could only pray that she had been seen. That one glimpse she had had been enough to terrify her. She wasn't drifting into the bay at all, but further out to sea!

Next stop Minorca! she told herself, trying to curb her rising hysteria before a passion of gratitude flooded through her. The powerful speedboat was edging its way towards her, the slap of its hull on the waves making her realise again just how rough the sea had become.

It wasn't going to be an easy job to save her, she could see that, and she had a horrid feeling that her rescuer might not be too interested in bothering with the board and sail. With anxious eyes she watched the boat being steered between her and the wind, and a rope was then thrown expertly at her.

'Attach it to the base of the sail!' came a shout, followed by another: 'Can you make it over the side?'

The sleek lines of the boat posed little problem for her as she pulled her surfboard alongside, then, pulling out the keel from the board, she swung herself on to the boat with comparative ease.

She wasn't given a chance to do anything other than give a gasp of relief before he called her over. 'Look, if you want me to try to save the board and sail, can you keep the nose of the boat on to the *faro*, the lighthouse up on that headland?' He waited a moment to make sure she was in a fit state to understand what he wanted of her. 'Got it?'

Exhausted and cold, she was only capable of nodding, as she held on to the wheel, desperate to keep the boat's nose facing that distant pinnacle, not even daring to check to see if her rescuer was being as good as his word. She had a nasty feeling that if she had to replace that board and sail it would take most of her summer's salary to do so.

When a pair of brown hands slid over the wheel she relinquished her hold and slipped down on to the deck behind him.

'I'm not going to be able to make it back to our bay, I'm afraid; we're going to have to head for the protection of the port!' she heard his voice shout above the wind. 'It's a bit rough, so I think you'd better stay where you are and try to hang on to your board. We don't want to lose it again, do we?' He didn't turn his head; his whole concentration seemed to be on keeping the boat under control.

Jane apprehensively tried to do what he suggested. A considerable amount of water was being shipped, and there was a very real problem that the board, which was too big and unwieldy to fit comfortably in the limited space, would disappear over the side. It wasn't exactly a comfortable position to be in, but then she had to admit it was better than her previous one. After all, whoever owned this boat was her saviour. Heaven only knew what would have happened if he hadn't seen her. She owed him a great deal more than gratitude. Why, he even spoke English, for heaven's sake! Her Spanish was English A level standard, and, although fairly fluent in normal circumstances, she wasn't sure in her present predicament whether it would have completely deserted her.

She took several deep breaths, trying to control the weakness of her limbs as she said a silent prayer.

'Here!' A brown hand tossed a towel down to her. 'Sorry I can't help, but this sea's a bit too rough to be out in for comfort. That's why I couldn't tow the board and sail behind us.'

Gratefully Jane pulled the towel around her shoulders, trying at the same time to remove the worst of the tears and salt spray from her face. Ahead of her two long brown legs, slightly splayed to cope with the violent motion of the boat, moved easily with the bucking and jerking movements that made her content for the moment anyway to stay where she was. The faded blue espadrilles on his feet appeared anchored to the deck, which was all the more remarkable because she was having great difficulty in trying to stop herself, the board and sail becoming mixed up in some sort of general mêlée.

He wore cotton checked knee-length shorts belted at the waist, with a thin blue cotton shirt so fine that she could see the lean brown body beneath. Wow! she thought. If that's the back view then I can't wait for him to turn round! Sunglasses, and a preoccupation with her own troubles, had ensured that she'd had nothing but the most fleeting glimpse of this man who had come so providentially to her aid. Beyond the fact that he spoke English, was comparatively young, and that he had to have spent a great deal of time outdoors to have gained such a fantastic tan, she might not even recognise him if he walked past her in a street.

So she stayed where she was, not caring that the position was hardly dignified, until the stranger brought the boat into the lee of the big bay. The almost instantaneous effect this had on the waves had her scrambling to her feet.

Well, that was a relief, she told herself, and as there didn't seem to be any danger of losing the board any more then there was no reason for her to suffer either. The luxuriously padded seats looked extremely tempting, but she'd got her timing wrong, because at the same moment he hit the throttle, and the surge of power once more had her thrown back rather painfully on to her bottom.

'Sorry about that. I didn't realise you were on the move!' He turned round, and she was treated to a view of even white teeth as he grinned at the tangle her legs seemed to have got into. 'I'm going to be late for a date, thanks to you!' He leant backwards to give her a hand up. 'You'd better sit down properly!' He gestured towards one of the softly padded seats beside him, and somewhat uncertainly she sat down on it, having managed to tie his towel around her skimpy swimsuit.

The powerful boat zapped its way across the bay, slapping its hull down on the still occasional big waves and causing at least one of its passengers to review her feelings about speedboats and their drivers, let alone the extreme discomfort of travelling in one without adequate cushioning to combat the effect of being thrown up and down on what she had thought would be an improvement on the teak deck. Well, of course it was comfier, but the boat was leaping from wave to wave with such force that she could only be glad she wasn't still sitting on the deck holding on to the surfboard, which was thumping up and down in sympathy as she gave it apprehensive glances.

'Relax! You won't lose it now, I promise. You know, you are damn lucky I saw you leave the bay! I was watching to see the speedboat didn't hit you,' he told her. 'Most people have their siesta in the afternoon. I realise you might find that a little difficult to adjust to, particularly if you are only here for a short time, but it's no bad thing to rest in the heat of the day. If you'd gone out this morning you'd probably have been perfectly OK, but that sail is too heavy for you! Hans was an idiot not to have warned you.'

Jane couldn't help resenting his words. The phrase ''handsome is as handsome does'' floated into the periphery of her mind. Of course, it was slightly difficult to overlook the fact that he'd just rescued her from—what? An uncomfortable few hours at sea? Anyway, it certainly wouldn't have been death, she reminded herself, so she'd no need to go overboard with gratitude. He'd obviously written her off as someone of no particular importance; a tourist perhaps who had come for a traditional two-week break to the only hotel on the small bay, one that catered for package holidays at the lower end of the range. She swelled slightly with indignation. 'I'm a lot stronger than I look!' she told him indignantly. 'And anyway, Hans did warn me...' It hurt to admit that she'd been wrong.

'I'm sure you are!' he teased, his white teeth flashing at her in a grin. 'But it's better not to overestimate one's strength, particularly when one is dealing with anything so unpredictable and capricious as the sea.'

Being forced into accepting that he was right didn't make her feel any better. There was something about the faintly patronising tone of his voice that unfortunately brought out the worst in her. He was treating her as if she were little better than a teenage idiot, when in point of fact she was twenty-two years old and, most of the time, perfectly capable of looking after herself.

After a severe struggle with herself, she managed to say politely, 'Thank you for your advice. I'll certainly remember next time to take more care.'

'You'd do well to do so!' This time he took off his dark glasses to smile at her properly, but his dark eyes were still amused as she considered the totally unfair length of his eyelashes.

She knew it was rude to stare, but she couldn't help herself. She'd been so convinced that he was an Englishman, it was rather hard to accept that she had been wrong about that as well, because her rescuer just had to be Spanish after all. Tall, elegant and just faintly intimidating, with that air of confident assurance that came of being either very grand or very rich, or even perhaps both. Jet-black brows above the dark eyes, and a mobile mouth that was twisted up with amusement at her expression.

'I thought you were English!' she blurted out.

'You're only half right, I'm afraid.' He had put his sunglasses back on, but his voice still smiled.

'How did you happen to see me go out of the bay?' she enquired suddenly. 'I thought it would be Hans who'd be checking up on me.'

'Let's just say you were lucky I was checking up on someone else until I got side-tracked...'

Jane wasn't sure she liked his answer, or the grin on his face. She guessed he'd been studying her through binoculars, and, not wanting to pursue the subject, she changed tack.

'Was it your mother or your father?' she demanded, rather disjointedly, it had to be admitted.

For a moment he looked puzzled, then he laughed. 'You mean which of them was English?' She nodded. 'My mother was born in London... You should have realised that Hans is more interested in blonde fräuleins than you... You weren't on his mind until it was too late for him to take out his own boat. He was suitably grateful when I told him I was going to the rescue!'

They were slowing down as they entered the port, but to Jane's inexperienced eyes he still appeared to be going far too fast through the busy little marina as he made his way to what was obviously his own mooring. A young boy was waiting for them, and her companion threw him the rope to tie them up. The boy made the boat fast, then jumped down on to the deck. The two of them then began to speak in such rapid Spanish that Jane was pushed to keep up.

It wasn't until she was actually in the port that she realised just exactly what a mess she must look—her hair dishevelled in the extreme, a smeared face, and just her swimsuit. No T-shirt, pareu or shoes, nothing in fact to disguise the fact that she'd come straight from the sea—apart from his towel. It wasn't as if the port was a tiny, insignificant little place either—it was quite a sophisticated town.

No wonder too that her rescuer was treating her like a child, because that was what she must look like.

'Carlos, darling! You're quite shamefully late!'

Jane looked up with horror to see the angry face of quite one of the most tiresome girls she had ever had the misfortune to know standing waiting for them on the stone jetty. That was typical of fate, wasn't it? To wait until she was looking really awful, then to let her meet the one girl who would not only remark on her looks, but would also take pleasure from them.

Carlos leapt up on to the jetty, then put down a casual hand to help pull Jane up beside him before turning to greet the other girl with a placating smile on his face. 'Juanita. Yes, I know I'm late, but this time I have a genuine excuse. I had to rescue—er—sorry, I don't know your name?' Jane got another glimpse of white teeth before he turned away to lightly kiss the other girl's extended hand.

Juanita gave her a sour look. She was dressed simply in a white mini-skirt and a peach T-shirt which managed to look exactly right for her surroundings. 'Hi, Jane. What on earth are you doing here, and with Carlos? Your mother told me you were supposed to be working this summer.'

'Hi! I am,' Jane replied through gritted teeth. Judging by the way Juanita was clinging on to Carlos it was obvious she was making it clear that he belonged to her, and woe betide any trespassers! If there was one girl in the whole of Mallorca she'd have chosen not to see in her present state, it would have been Juanita de Tarrago. She had been spiteful and unkind as a girl, so it was hardly surprising she should have grown into a bitch. Jane had gone to what her family had thought of as excessive lengths to keep secret the fact that she was working on Mallorca for the summer, but now her secret was doubly blown, and to the one girl who she had intended never to know she was on the island.

'You two girls know each other?' The surprise on Carlos's face almost made her laugh, it was so comical. So she'd been right. He'd written her off as a little miss nobody—certainly not someone who could possibly know one of the richest girls in Spain.

Juanita gave him a tight little smile. 'We were at school together, that's all.'

A spirit of perversity made Jane raise her eyebrows.

'Why don't you tell him we're supposed to be best friends?' She gave Juanita a mock smile, its saccharine sweetness almost an insult in itself.

Juanita shrugged carelessly. 'I don't suppose it is of the slightest interest, is it, Carlos? Anyway——' she turned back to Jane '—I suppose you've been making a mess of things again. You never could take "no" for an answer, could you?

I suppose someone told you not to windsurf out of the bay, so, being Jane, you had to try and prove them wrong!' A real smile lit up her face as she saw the blush of mortification on Jane's face. 'Anyway, why on earth did you insist on coming out here and taking a job in the first place? You know I always want you to come and stay every summer...'

Jane forcibly swallowed everything she was tempted to say. Like she was fed up with playing the part of Juanita's stooge. Like... But she refused to allow her unruly thoughts to continue. She rustled up a polite smile. 'You know I like being independent, Juanita.'

'Yes—well, but isn't it carrying independence a bit far when your—er—"best friend" is refused even your address? Particularly,' Juanita continued, 'when you come to her country for a holiday.'

Jane shrugged her shoulders hopelessly. Juanita had never ever been able to see any point of view other than her own, and she had about as much finesse as a large tank in top gear when it came to overruling others' objections.

Carlos dug a hand into his pocket, bringing out a handful of pesetas. Jane thought he looked more than a little intrigued by her reluctance to get caught up with a member of the Tarrago family. He also ignored the look of mutinous refusal he could see forming on her face. 'Look, take a taxi back home. I really do have to get to a meeting now with Juanita. The board and sail will be quite safe here, and——' once more there was a glint of teeth '—you can thank me and pay me back tomorrow if you want to! OK?'

She was left with little choice, and, although it went against the grain, rather grudgingly she held out her hand. Lean brown fingers closed over it, slipping the pesetas neatly and discreetly into her palm, and, before she could protest, his lips lightly grazed the back of it. Her hand was steady under his touch, but she had to fight to keep it so, not wanting to betray any weakness before him. Anyway, who wanted anything to do with a man who was idiotic enough to be caught up with Juanita de Tarrago, even if he was unusually attractive? she told herself as she was left standing on the jetty watching the two of them head towards the white Mercedes with sun-darkened glass.

All through the rest of that busy day and the evening that followed, whenever she found herself thinking about Miguel, Jane firmly banished his image. Carlos now—he'd made it clear he was looking forward to seeing her the next day, but he'd done so in front of Juanita. Jane had very few illusions left about her. If anybody wanted character demolition done, then Juanita was more than equal to the job.

The two girls had met comparatively young. The friendship had started because Juanita had insisted on it, although her idea of friendship had been pretty strange to the English girl. Juanita's family treated her rather like a little princess, and if she wanted to make a great friend of the little English girl, then friend she would be, and she was invited out every summer to the Tarrago summer home on Mallorca. Juanita's older brother had also made her young life a misery by his teasing when she was younger, but the two Tarrago children were adept at hiding their behaviour from any adults who had happened to be around; well, certainly from any grown-ups who had mattered, Jane amended silently. Luckily, since she was seventeen Miguel had never been there at the same time as herself.

Jane had suffered from Juanita's attentions because she was prettier, although not cleverer, and, as far as devious manipulation went, she had been left standing. Juanita had wanted to be number one, always, and resented the fact that in spite of all her money Jane was inclined to be the more popular both with the girls and boys, even if it wasn't always admitted.

Juanita was head of a crowd who kow-towed to her because she was rich and powerful as well as having a spiteful tongue, and nothing had given her more pleasure than to bully her little so-called friend. It had been appalling bad luck that her family had sent her to an English convent to be educated, and even greater bad luck that they suffered the delusion that the two girls were great friends.

Jane's own family had been nearly as bad. Whenever they met Juanita she had been on her best behaviour, and her family thought Jane was really lucky to have such a good friend.

Although she had longed for it, Jane had never had quite the courage to complain to Juanita's mother about her behaviour, knowing that even if she had she wouldn't be believed. This was to have been the first holiday for years she would have had blessed relief from joining in the Tarrago holiday in Mallorca. Increasingly she had become upset at not working in the summer between university terms like nearly all the other students. Also, she'd felt it was time to break loose from the Tarrago hold. After all, it wasn't as if she and Juanita had ever been true friends, she told herself.

Now she'd left with her quite respectable degree, she hadn't been able to resist taking this summer job before she started to work in earnest in September. Cooking had always interested her, and she did it very well, in spite of only ever having had a six-week course. Of course, it had been maddening that the job was on Mallorca, and so close to Juanita's home, but then she would never have met Lady Waters if she hadn't been staying with the Tarragos in the first place.

In all those summers, this had been the first chance that she'd had to be able to learn to windsurf. Juanita learnt to play tennis because her father had insisted on it, and could water-ski, but any other sport left her cold, and what she didn't want to do nobody did. It had maddened Jane in the past, and perhaps had partly explained her obsessive keenness to learn to windsurf in the first place.

All through the evening she cooked virtually on auto-pilot, her thoughts tied up with Miguel, Juanita and Carlos, half knowing that Juanita would call her the following day to issue explicit instructions to leave Carlos alone; but which would call first?

It had happened so many times to her in the past—some boy becoming friendly, perhaps too friendly, until Juanita managed to break it up. It was a depressing fact that Jane had learned to live with. In Juanita's court money was the ultimate power, and it had sickened Jane many times to see how absolutely effective it was, over children as well as adults. Good looks, niceness of character— neither stood a chance against a girl who had so much money.

It had made Jane deeply cynical about people's motives. She had made the mistake, her first summer at university, of inviting a young man to join her in Mallorca. Juanita was always asking her to bring a friend, and in taking David with her Jane had been sure she was quite safe.

If not quite a card-carrying Communist, then he had been sufficiently left-wing to deeply despise Juanita and her family. It had taken forty-eight hours for Juanita and her lifestyle to seduce him from his beliefs. Jane's deep scorn at the speed of what she saw as his sell-out completely ruined that relationship, much to Juanita's ill-concealed amusement.

Jane herself hadn't been too amused either when David had accused her also of having sold out years ago. It had proved to be impossible to convey to him just exactly how difficult it had been for a child to refuse something so wonderful and yet so innocuous as a holiday abroad with a friend from school.

Although she was really, really tired at the end of that evening, she did come to one important decision. If Carlos got in touch with her before Juanita tomorrow, then, for the first time in her life, she'd try to give her a run for her money. It wouldn't do Miguel any harm either to realise that she was not at the Tarragos' beck and call. If he saw her with someone like Carlos he might even sit up and take a bit of real notice of her for a change.

After all, Carlos looked sufficiently wealthy to be independent, and Jane knew he was interested in her. He hadn't even bothered to disguise it in front of Juanita. In a way David had been right when he'd accused her of selling out too. Just by not fighting her she'd been guilty too. She might lose, but, from her first quick sight of it, the prize looked worth fighting for!

CHAPTER TWO

JANE was staggering into the kitchen on the first of her journeys from the car with the proceeds of Tuesday's big market shop when she heard the phone. Without hurrying, almost sure she knew who would be calling, she picked it up.

'Hello?'

'Good morning, Miss Mayfield, or may I, now we've been introduced, call you Jane?'

'Hi! Yes, call me Jane, please, but it was a pretty incomplete introduction, wasn't it? I still don't know your name, apart from Carlos, that is...'

It was difficult to try to keep her excitement at hearing from him flooding her voice. Suddenly the day had become interesting, but she didn't want him to know the reasons why she felt like that. No, that wouldn't be a good policy at all, would it? Men, anyway, were inclined not to value anything that came too easily. Still, it shouldn't be too hard not letting him know that the sound of his voice had her fizzing with excitement at her future plans.

She heard his laughter. 'I'm sorry, I thought Juanita would have rung you last night. I'm Carlos Vilafranca; I live most of the year here in Mallorca where my family have been based for very many years——'

28

'Lucky you!' she interrupted. 'Listen, Carlos, I'm really grateful for what you did yesterday, but I'm rather busy at the moment. I've just come back from the market . . .'

'Of course, I forgot! How stupid of me—you are working. Listen, don't worry about the board and sail; they will be returned to Hans today.'

'Oh, please, could you take them back this morning?' asked Jane. 'You see, I expect he'll charge me for the time . . .'

'Oh, no, he won't! He's already been ticked off for not checking on you carefully enough.'

'But I did go out against his wishes!' she protested feebly.

'Even so, it is part of his job to help people who get into trouble with his equipment. You had a bad fright yesterday, and that was unnecessary. So! Are you free in the afternoons?'

'Yes.' She couldn't help smiling a little in anticipation, wondering what he would suggest.

'Would you like to come out in the boat with me? I know a small bay which is very beautiful and still undeveloped, so it is clean and peaceful. We could swim, or you could water-ski if you want to.'

'Sounds fun!' She knew he would be able to hear the smile in her voice. 'But what about your siesta?'

'I'm prepared to give it up today for the pleasure of your company! Will you be free by three o'clock?' he asked.

'I should be. Although lunch is late, we don't really keep Spanish hours here,' Jane told him.

'Good. See you later, then.' He rang off, leaving her to smile like an idiot among the big baskets full of sweet-smelling melons, beef tomatoes and all the other fresh vegetables that she'd spent the last couple of hours buying in the market.

There! So much for her trying not to appear too available. She couldn't help feeling pleased, though, because Carlos hadn't wasted much time in getting in touch with her. There was no denying that she'd been feeling a little afraid that Juanita might have managed to put him off making any move towards her at all.

She knew so well how Juanita worked; the little hints, the innuendoes, but nothing overt, so that it was never possible to get hold of anything concrete to deny. It was a process Jane had seen repeated and refined so often over the years that unwillingly she had almost come to admire it even when it had been used against her to devastating effect.

She pulled herself together. It was no good, as her grandmother used to tell her, to cross bridges before she came to them, but forewarned was forearmed. Juanita would have been out all night at one of the local discos, and Jane would have been surprised to hear that she was home before five or six in the morning; therefore she had at least until midday to plan how to be beyond the reach of a phone when she called.

Lady Waters would have to be told that anyone who called her between eleven in the morning and three in the afternoon would find her unavailable.

When she put this idea to her boss a little later, however, she looked doubtful.

'Really, Jane, if Juanita wants to talk to you I don't see how I can refuse her,' she said.

Jane knew that Lady Waters' Achilles' heel lay in her stomach. She and her husband were extremely fond of their food. It wasn't that they wanted exotic cooking—oh, no... They wanted good plain cooking that used to advantage the local vegetables, and that required painstaking preparation. Sir Dick, as he was affectionately known, had had a heart attack a few years previously, so he preferred to eat healthily.

'I like to know what's on my plate, my dear!' he had told Jane at her interview. 'I can't stand things buried in a sauce. Use your imagination, pick the best Mediterranean cooking, then go on from there—that's the secret of good cooking! I can't stand some of these cordon-bleu trained girls, always having to do everything exactly as it says in the recipe book, and using no imagination whatsoever! Cooking is, and should be, a creative art...'

So far she'd managed to please them both, and their guests, but Jane frowned a little at Lady Waters' words.

'I don't think Juanita realises that I'm taking my job here with you very seriously,' she said. 'I'm afraid that if she gets on the phone—well, she'll want to talk for ages, and I won't be able to do lunch. I thought it would be easiest for all of us if we said I was busy at those times, so maybe she could leave a message.'

'I see . . .' Lady Waters frowned back. 'Yes, that could be a problem.'

Jane continued, 'Juanita doesn't really understand that people, ordinary people, that is, have to work for a living. I mean, most of her friends are free like her, so she may find it difficult to accept that I'm different. That's why I didn't want her to know I was here, but as she found out yesterday— well, it seems to me that this is the best answer.'

'Yes, yes . . . Well, we certainly can't have her spoiling lunch, that's for sure!' Lady Waters gave Jane a rather doubtful smile as she drifted out of the kitchen, leaving a thoughtful girl behind her. So Lady Waters didn't want to risk offending the Tarragos, even if that meant upsetting the cook? Sir Dick was known as a "captain of industry"— perhaps that meant he had important dealings with the Tarrago family? Certainly she knew that their interests extended far beyond Spain.

Quietly she went on working, although she still couldn't help thinking about the power of money and even more if she had been wise to accept this job in the first place. She ought to have known that Juanita would be bound to find out where she was.

Another thought, quite startling in its intensity, filled her mind. She had known Juanita would find her—had wanted her to, so she could prove to her and her brother once and for all that they had no power over her, and never had had.

The truth of this hit her with an immediacy that made her catch her breath in protest. For years she'd resented being a sort of unofficial lady-in-waiting who'd lacked the guts to walk away from the situation. To compensate, she'd become over-aggressive in other fields, always trying desperately hard to succeed on her own behalf without any-one's help.

She'd resented Miguel's teasing attentions to herself, and the way he'd been all too easily sur-rounded by pretty girls—Juanita's friends, as well as the international beauties that his great fortune attracted. She had spent five years trying to con-vince herself it was money that was his only attraction.

Once she had recovered from the shock of this discovery about herself, she also found out that her desire to take Carlos away from Juanita had grown from idle thoughts about an attractive man into a firm resolve to put Juanita and her brother in their place. If she was ever to regain her own self-respect then this was a battle that had to be fought from her own meagre armoury of natural assets against the big guns of unlimited money and power. She knew that she hadn't really a hope in upsetting Miguel, but he was fond of his sister, and maybe, just maybe, it might make him remember that he had found her attractive once.

Jane had been quite right. Juanita had rung, and had been most insistent about talking to her, but luckily Sir Dick had answered the phone, and he was obviously made of sterner stuff than his wife, because he had been equally insistent that Juanita just leave a message. Luckily this had been no more than that she'd called, and would call again that evening.

Jane waited for Carlos on the jetty below the villa in a fever of anxiety. Juanita, balked of her prey, could well be on her way round to the villa now in the beautiful boat that Jane had seen Miguel in yesterday, and which was usually used to ferry her and her friends around the coast.

She relaxed her vigilance when she saw Carlos's boat, the *Viviana*, making its way across the bay to pick her up. Already Hans had come over to apologise for yesterday's disaster. Jane had assured him that it was her own fault, not his, so they had parted friends, even though she had had to ignore his unspoken innuendo that he had somehow done her a favour by sending Carlos out to find her. She knew he would probably be even more outspoken after he'd seen the *Viviana* come and collect her from the jetty this afternoon.

So keen was she to get away that she wasted little time in scrambling on to the boat, falling ungracefully on to the foredeck in the process, before Carlos had even properly come alongside.

'I've never had a girl quite this keen for my company before!' Carlos teased, as he eased them slowly away. 'Or didn't you want me to meet any of your companions?' he added in a whisper.

Jane laughed, but she couldn't help blushing also as she waved goodbye to the middle-aged couple who were working up their tans while trying to ignore several persistent holiday-makers from the beach who were trying to heave themselves up on the jetty to join them, in spite of its clearly appearing to be private property and only reached from the villa above.

Shameful though it was to leave him thinking it was her eagerness to be with him, she decided that it would be prudent not to be truthful.

'I was a bit worried about those swimmers trying to get on the jetty,' she answered, a little lamely. 'I mean, you could have had an accident and hit one of them or something ...' Keen to change the subject before he could tease her further, she continued, 'Which of the villas over there is yours?'

'You can't really see it too well from here because of the pine trees, but it's that one.'

He pointed to a distant low wall to the right of the small beach opposite them, and she just caught glimpses of dazzling white through the trees.

'I see what you mean, or rather I don't see!' she laughed back at him, then relaxed, as the boat surged out of the small bay without there being any sign of Juanita. Now she was free to concentrate on herself and her immediate surroundings. She congratulated herself on her good taste as she studied Carlos discreetly but carefully—blue and white long cotton swimming-trunks and just the espadrilles on his feet. His back was as smooth and lean as polished walnut, but his chest was covered in dark hair which narrowed at his waistline to plunge unseen to areas hidden by his swimsuit. In fact, looking at him dispassionately, Jane could quite understand Juanita's interest, and she wondered why he didn't also make her heart beat faster.

She too was wearing something in blue, but hers was a bikini with touches of red in it, the top in a flattering underwired bra with gentle pleats, and the bottom with high-cut legs and a chevron-shaped wrap-over front. Designed not to come adrift when diving, it was pretty as well as practical. Jane was not interested in the minimalistic look, even if she'd had the courage to wear it. She believed her father, who'd always told her nudity was a turn-off for men, most of them preferring to use their imaginations to explore the bits left covered.

Because she wasn't very tall she always tried to wear cork block-soled slip-ons to add to her height. Today she had her short hair tidied neatly; she wanted to show Carlos that she didn't always look such a mess as when he'd found her yesterday. Her blue beach bag contained make-up for running repairs as well as a comb, and a long cotton T-shirt to slip over her bikini if she got cold, as well as a towel.

Because the sea had miraculously sunk back to just a gentle swell she found she was enjoying roaring out to sea, and wondered how far they were going. The long open sands of Canyamel weren't far away, she knew, but Carlos cut the engine surprisingly quickly and the *Viviana* slid smoothly around the rocky headland into a tiny and completely private little bay very close to their own.

'Why, this is lovely!' Jane exclaimed. 'And it's not really so far away, is it?'

'Just far enough to deter any but the strongest of swimmers,' he agreed. *Viviana* settled gracefully back down on to the water like a swan coming into land, while Carlos leisurely climbed forward to drop the anchor. The water was so clear that Jane watched the anchor sink to the bottom, where it rested on a patch of sand. The absolute quiet after the powerful noises of the engine was wonderful, and gradually, as her ears adjusted to the silence, she became aware of the lapping of the water against the boat, the gentle hiss of the waves as they curled whitely over the black rocks that ringed the shore.

'That's one of the reasons why it has escaped development.' Carlos pointed once more to the rocks. 'Saved because there's no beach!'

'I don't like sand very much myself,' Jane answered thoughtfully. 'If I ever had the money to build myself a house in the sun, I'd choose some-where like here.'

The tiny bay enclosed them in glittering shimmers of light as the sun danced off the blue and green sea. 'Why does the sea sometimes look green?' Jane enquired lightly, pointing down at the patch be-neath them that glowed with all the colour of an emerald in contrast to the deeper sapphire near by.

'Because we're anchored over sand,' Carlos told her. 'Don't you know about blue and yellow mixed?' he teased.

'Make green!' she answered. 'How stupid! I never thought of that before.'

'Well, I'm not sure if that's the real answer; that's just my theory. Are you ready to swim?' Carlos queried. 'There's a grotto over on that side—a small one, it's true, but it's rather fun to explore. I've brought masks as well.'

'I'd love to!' Jane said, her grey eyes brilliant with excitement. 'But it's so clear today that masks hardly seem necessary.'

'Yes, we're lucky. The waves yesterday could have stirred up the bottom. Look! Do you see? Over there?'

He leant close to her, one arm pointing, and Jane found his sudden closeness so uncomfortable that she found it difficult to concentrate. A picture of Miguel looking at her with a frown came into her mind with accusing rapidity, which she found rather extraordinary until she managed to banish it. Why should Carlos sitting next to her have prompted that image? she wondered. Either way, she refused to speculate further on the workings of her mind. The sudden shower of tiny leaping silver fish disturbed the water in front of them, and then, bobbing to the surface, with one fish idiotically hanging sideways out of his beak, was the only other inhabitant of the bay.

'Oh, it's the cormorant! He comes fishing in our bay as well, doesn't he? I always wondered where he went to...'

'You've seen him before?' One dark eyebrow was raised in a query.

'Yes...' Her voice sounded a little strangled to her, and she cleared her throat while trying unobtrusively to put a little more of a gap between their bodies. 'He swims off the rocks near our villa.'

She had the uncomfortable feeling that Carlos was reading the wrong messages into her reactions, or were they the right ones? Ambivalent though she was about her feelings for him, was he somehow taking advantage of it as his dark eyes smiled into hers? Her grey eyes still bravely held his brown ones, but she couldn't help wondering if her ideas of getting involved with this good-looking stranger were going to take her out of her depth—and this was before her little game had even started!

'Hey, what's the matter? You look sad all of a sudden!' Carlos smiled to lighten the mood between them. 'Race you to that rock out there! You get ten seconds' start, starting right now!'

Jane was absurdly grateful for the sudden change of atmosphere. Although why she should have found herself feeling so uncertain with such an attractive man was beyond her. Without wasting a second, and on the count of 'One!', she had dived cleanly off the boat and was swimming in a fast crawl towards the goal.

He caught her just as her hand was reaching out to touch it, and pulled her back against his lean strength.

'You really thought you had it made then, didn't you?' he teased.

'Yes, I did!' She shook the water from her face, and grinned before relaxing against him. As she did so, his hold on her loosened and she was able to make her escape, until he caught her again.

That became the pattern of the afternoon: light-hearted play that each seemed determined should extend to their feelings for each other. Both of them seemed intent on keeping the new relationship light, with the emphasis on fun, as they slowly began to know each other through the drowsy heat of that first long afternoon alone together.

'I must get back,' Jane told him lazily as she rolled over on to her tummy. He followed suit, his roll exaggerated by the movement of the boat over the swell, so his body now lay touching the length of hers. She sat up and clasped her knees, trying to ignore the expression of sleepy appreciation on Carlos's face as he looked at her. His brown eyes were full of mischief, the sun setting light to little gold devils that seemed to dance merrily in the dark depths.

Jane felt the muscles of her tummy contract in response to that unspoken invitation that shimmered in the air between them.

'Must you go?' he asked her lazily, and she didn't need his oblique message to be spelt out to her. So why this hesitation on her part? Wasn't this exactly what she wanted?

It was the return of the cormorant that brought her to her senses. Perched on a nearby rock, he opened his beak to give a loud, protesting call, keeping one beady black eye fixed balefully on them. She couldn't help laughing, and Carlos joined in, albeit ruefully, a little later.

'That bird has a great deal to answer for!' he told her, as he started to pull in the anchor. 'He spoiled a beautiful moment!' But Jane was still laughing with relief. The situation had been taken out of her hands.

'Oh, no! We've just outstayed our welcome as far as he's concerned, that's all!' she asserted.

'He'd better watch it! This bay belongs to me.'

Jane turned to look at him with interest. 'Does it really?' she asked.

He smiled at her, before starting up the engine, the exhaust bubbling throatily, drawing yet another protest from the black cormorant. 'Oh, yes,' he said. 'Most of the land around here does, you know.' He ignored her expression of round-eyed surprise. 'My family have owned land on Mallorca for hundreds of years. Of course, for most of that time it has just simply been farmland, the coastal areas of no particular importance compared to the fertile plains inland; but the coming of the tourists changed all that!' He gave her a quick, almost impersonal look. 'Do you want to water-ski back into the bay?'

She shook her head. 'No, thanks, Carlos, not today. I've had a fantastic afternoon, thank you very much. Restful after all the excitements of yesterday, and just what I needed!'

'Would you like to repeat it?' he asked.

'Well, yes, of course I would! Thanks.'

'Not at all. Perhaps, the next time, we could do something a bit more ambitious—say on your day off?'

Jane didn't try to hide her smile. 'Now that really sounds fun, Carlos.'

'Good! So when are you free?'

'Thursday—the day after tomorrow.'

'Even better. We can go out all day, then spend the evening at Juanita's party.'

'Juanita's party?' She made little pretence at hiding her dismay.

'Yes, didn't you know? It's to celebrate Miguel's, her brother's, thirtieth birthday. It should be the best party on the island all summer. Everyone will be there, you'll see!'

'But I thought... I mean, I heard he's already had a party in Madrid,' Jane queried.

'He did. This is just an informal one that's being organised by Juanita, but I'm not sure it won't be more fun, don't you think? Anyway, I've been helping her. She wanted fireworks, and that's what we were doing yesterday.'

'She may not want me to be there...' Jane tried again.

'Nonsense! She was thrilled you were on the island. I'm only amazed she hasn't been in touch with you yet.'

'She did try this morning, but I couldn't talk because I was working.' Carlos didn't appear to notice that she was hardly enthusiastic, perhaps because he found it hard to believe. The Tarrago parties were famous all over Europe, attracting the rich and the famous, all the beautiful people in droves. People had been known to go to absurd lengths just to get invitations, so perhaps it was hardly surprising he found Jane's reluctance to believe herself a guest unbelievable.

The *Viviana* rounded the headland back into what she thought of as their own bay, with Jane now absurdly full of relief that soon she would be alone to think things out. It was extraordinary how quickly her mood had changed; even the man standing next to her in the boat seemed to lose his importance a little as she grappled with the news of Juanita's party for Miguel.

Miguel! Everything always came back to Miguel. The one who had tried, the last time the three of them spent a summer together, to make her fall for him. When she had first been aware that his teasing attentions towards her had subtly changed she wasn't quite sure, but whenever he was around she'd been filled with a sort of dangerous excitement. That had culminated in a kiss of such dangerous, searing passion that if she hadn't run away, frightened of the feelings he'd invoked in her, heaven knew what would have happened. She had been furiously resentful of his power to make her feel so hot and ashamed in his presence.

When he'd gone early the next day, without a word to her, she'd been left with such a maelstrom of feelings that she'd told herself countless times that she was happy neither to have seen nor heard from him since—until the day before yesterday.

She had always been aware, though, of his reputation as an international lover of beautiful women. Sometimes she had felt complimented that he'd tried and failed to make her one of his girlfriends, other times she had felt scornfully dismissive of his blatant affairs.

Jane, while reasonably sure that he would long have grown out of any interest he might have had in her when she was seventeen, was still not madly keen to meet him again, particularly after his eyes had teased her so relentlessly yesterday. He had proved himself painfully immune to her charms five years ago, and she wasn't going to let him trample over her dreams again just to prove he was irresistible. He could boost his ego with his blonde companion, not her, so she was silent as Carlos brought the boat around to lie against the jetty. He even had to prompt her, so lost in her own thoughts was she.

'I'm sorry!' Big grey eyes looked up at him. 'I was miles away, dreaming!'

'I forgive you! So we have a date on Thursday?'

'Yes, please!' she smiled.

'Weather permitting, which way would you rather go?' he asked. 'North or south?'

'I'd like to go north, if you don't mind, because I love that part of the coast,' she told him.

'North it is! And if the weather forecast's not too good as far as the boat is concerned, then I'll take you by car. OK?'

'OK!' she smiled. 'And thank you—I've really enjoyed my afternoon.'

'*De nada*!' Carlos held the boat steady as she leapt lightly on to the now empty jetty. Apart from a brief smile, she didn't wait to see him leave, but just ran across the heavy wooden planks towards the steps that led up to the villa.

She wasn't given much time to be alone in her room before she was called to the phone. Mentally she tried to brace herself against what was to come.

'Jane? Where have you been?' demanded Juanita. 'I expected you to call me back ages ago.' The familiar tones had Jane gritting her teeth in resentment.

'Hi! Sorry I wasn't able to talk earlier.'

'Where have you been? I came round to the Waters' villa this afternoon, but I was told you'd gone off in somebody's boat.'

'Yes,' said Jane. 'I was out with Carlos.'

'Carlos? Carlos Vilafranca?' Jane smiled to herself at the sound of outrage in Juanita's voice.

'Yes. What's wrong with that?' she enquired innocently. 'He invited me to go with him. He seems quite keen to get to know me better!' she finished—a little smugly, it had to be admitted. Jane knew she had disconcerted Juanita by the length of time she was taking to answer her seemingly innocent question.

'I don't think you can know that Carlos is a particular friend of mine!' the other girl told her stiffly.

'Yes, he told me he was,' Jane answered happily. 'Also that he'd been helping you to organise a party for Miguel. He seemed to think that you'd naturally want me to be there now you've found out I'm on the island.' Now this was a quite deliberate ploy on Jane's part to get an admission from Juanita that she was not wanted at the party, and for a moment she thought she had succeeded, but Juanita didn't fall into the trap.

'Naturally both Miguel and I are looking forward to seeing you on Thursday evening,' Juanita answered in a stiff little voice. 'He sounded quite pleased this morning when he told me you were on the island. He used to fancy you when he was younger; do you remember?' Her voice had taken on a note of sly amusement as she continued. 'You upset the family—they didn't think that was at all suitable! That's why the two of you didn't meet again when you came to stay with me!' She laughed. 'I expect you'll find it harder to get his interest now, although, knowing you, I expect you'll still try to attract his attention somehow, just as you used to do in the old days!'

Jane's hurt at Juanita's cruel reminder threatened to spill over into intemperate speech. Oh, how she longed to tell Juanita how many times Miguel's teasing had driven her to tears of frustration, but she knew her fury would let the other girl know she'd scored a hit, so with difficulty she swallowed her feelings in a laugh. 'I'm quite sure Miguel has outgrown me, but it will be amusing to see him again, even if it is only briefly. Anyway, Carlos has already promised to look after me!' Saccharine-sweet, she hoped that would put Juanita in her place, but her enemy was back on form.

'Great! I'll make sure the two of you get together, then Carlos won't have to waste his time being kind to you. Anyway, I gather from Miguel that you are the only girl who's ever turned him down flat. No wonder he's still intrigued by you! Perhaps this party of mine will really turn out to be the start of something exciting between you!' said Juanita.

'Don't get his hopes up!' Jane couldn't help snapping. 'Tell him I haven't changed my views over the intervening years.'

Juanita laughed in excitement. 'A boy-and-girl romance, spoiled by family disapproval! Why, Jane, if you play your cards right, who knows? One day you might end up my sister!'

'Don't get too carried away, Juanita! Miguel could hardly be described as a boy five years ago. Also, if your family thought I was unsuitable then, they'll hardly have changed their ideas in five years!' It hurt, it really hurt to have Juanita put into words what she'd always half suspected. Indeed, if the truth were known, it was Miguel's rejection of her that had really poisoned her mind against the Tarragos.

'Why, whatever gave you that idea?' Juanita laughed. 'Nobody has ever thought that about you, certainly not Mamá or Papá. You do jump to the wrong conclusions, don't you? No, everyone disapproved because you were so young! Even Miguel agreed that it was better if you grew up a bit before he met you again.'

'I wish you'd stop building up these little pictures in your mind.' Jane was disbelieving of Juanita's excuses. 'I know we're friends, but I don't think he's going to be too interested in your little friend from school. You're forgetting all those beautiful blonde models!'

'Oh, those!' Juanita's tone was heavily dismissive. 'They don't mean anything serious—you ought to know that! All men like to flirt with pretty girls before they settle down. Why, look at Carlos. I expect he made it clear he was interested in having a good time, didn't he? He's rather good at chatting up girls, but he's never serious. He's still far too interested in enjoying himself...'

Jane, knowing she'd already made a tactical error over Miguel, and because Juanita had hurt her, was intent on fighting back. 'I'm not sure you're right about Carlos,' she said. 'I think maybe that could have been true, but my guess is a clever girl could get him to settle down fairly soon if she played her cards right.' She laughed again. 'Anyway, if he's picked me for a summer playmate, I'm not complaining. We had a really nice time together this afternoon, and we're spending the day together on Thursday...'

There was a little silence before Juanita said, 'Don't blight Miguel's hopes before he's even had a chance with you, will you, darling? After all, I'd have thought even you would think twice—he's supposed to be such an attractive man! Anyway, I'm really thrilled to have found you, even if you are skulking away like a mouse in its hole. Come over early on Thursday, won't you? We've got a lot of catching up to do. *Adiós*!'

Jane put the phone down thoughtfully, aware that she'd allowed Juanita to wrong-foot her twice. How stupid to have told her that she and Carlos were spending Thursday together! She was fairly sure that Juanita would manage to sabotage that little outing without too much difficulty.

Just for a moment all the old feelings of hopelessness rose up and threatened to swamp her. It would be so much easier to let go. After all, what had she and Carlos to regret? Nothing at the moment, except his awareness of her, which she might be able to make grow into something interesting, or closer acquaintance could fade into a mirage of what-might-have-beens on his part.

Now she was committed to go to the party, and, if what she remembered of Miguel was still true, would have to fend off his teasing advances on her person. Juanita was right; he hadn't liked being turned down by his sister's little English schoolfriend. When she'd fought herself free of his embrace that first time, he'd caught her back, pulling her body so close to his that she'd felt the heat of his arousal.

'See what you do to me, little one!' he had whispered in her ear, but she'd been far too shy to confess that it had also excited her almost unbearably. She also knew from something Juanita had told her earlier that day that it meant nothing important to him.

'Miguel's told me that a man can want a woman terribly and it is nothing to do with love! So, Jane, be careful of my brother. I think he is too much of a man for you to handle...' Her sly smile of amusement had infuriated Jane at the time.

'You Tarragos! You think you can have everything you want, but your brother won't get me, because I won't let him!' she had answered fiercely, and that had been why she'd run away from him. She had never even admitted to herself that it was her emotions she was afraid of. She blamed the whole stupid muddle of her mixed-up feelings on Miguel, not even admitting that nothing in the last five years had ever come near to knocking her sideways like the memory of his kiss.

So she stood in front of the long mirror in her room, tidying herself in preparation for the evening ahead, half wondering if she'd made a dreadful mistake by so obviously challenging Juanita. The other girl had always relished the little fights, the power struggles that had gone on between them, but Jane knew that this was something altogether bigger, something that could have far-reaching consequences for them all. She'd thrown down her gauntlet, and it had been eagerly picked up. Just for a moment Jane wondered if Juanita had really fallen in love with Carlos, but then she rejected that thought. Her monstrous egotism would surely allow her to love no one but herself.

What about Carlos, whom she had cast in the role of innocent pawn in this diversion of hers? Would he be content to stay in his allotted role, or would he try to become a leading character in this chess game of human emotions that she'd set up?

Carlos… As she remembered those lazy dark eyes that had caressed her body all afternoon, Jane knew with pleasure that she had the means to humiliate Juanita at last; to make her see that she wasn't just a little nobody who could be kicked around by either the brother or the sister. Perhaps, at long last, she had it in her power to put them both in their place.

CHAPTER THREE

JANE had been on tenterhooks the whole of Wednesday, expecting to hear from either Juanita or Carlos that Thursday's plans had been changed, but mysteriously she heard nothing. Still in a state of suspended belief, she had had a shower and now stood wrapped in a towel, undecided what she should wear.

Admittedly, the choice was fairly limited considering she was planning to spend the whole day with Carlos in the boat. In the end she decided on her bikini, her shorts and a T-shirt and her Reeboks, just in case there was some sightseeing to be done. In her present state she found it a relief to concentrate on inessentials such as clothes.

As far as she could tell the weather looked good, but then she was no expert. At least Carlos didn't seem the type who would risk everything just to impress, she decided as she spooned herself a mouthful of melon, which was all she found she could face for breakfast today because she felt so fidgety and on edge.

'Oh, there you are, my dear!' Lady Waters smiled as she walked into the kitchen. 'Although I'd have thought you spent enough time in here to avoid it on your days off!'

Jane laughed politely, but found she wasn't able to think of anything remotely possible to answer that didn't sound very rude.

'Carlos Vilafranca rang and left a message for you. I gather you're spending the day with him?' Jane nodded. 'How nice! I do think he's a charming man ... Now where was I? Oh, yes, the message. He wants to know if you can make your own way down to the port. He seemed to think you'd know where the boat is berthed,' Lady Waters finished comfortably. 'I'm ready to go to the market myself, so you can get a lift with me if you want to. You may be a little early, but I expect that'll be better than waiting for the bus, won't it?'

'Thank you very much—yes, of course it is,' Jane agreed, but already she was trying to work out what lay behind Carlos's change of plan as she gathered her things together.

Abandoned by her boss near the port, Jane continued on foot until it came into view. She dawdled then, knowing she was a good half an hour too early for Carlos's rendezvous. She decided to have a coffee while she sat and waited.

The strength of the sun promised another very hot day, and she was grateful that she had already tanned sufficiently for it not to be too much of a problem, although she had put on a sun-block. A large straw hat shaded her face, allowing the sun shining through the weave to make interesting patterns on her cheeks.

'Well, well, well, what a charming sight! Not totally unexpected, I have to admit, but still charming. I have to admit you have hardly changed at all, *querida*!'

A tall shape stood between Jane and the sun, its very size somehow menacing as instinctively she shrank back in her chair, her grey eyes opened wide with shock as she tried to take in the enormity of having been found again by Miguel de Tarrago.

The scrape of metal on the pavement as he drew a chair to the table so he could join her, its jarring noise rasping her nerves nearly as badly as his presence, had her clinging to the table-top with fingers that had gone white under the strength of her grip.

'What are you doing here?' she demanded, her voice sounding suspicious. While he was not normally someone who danced the night away, even so it was unusual to find him in the port so early, and, even more unusual, alone.

Two thick black brows rose over a pair of wicked black eyes. 'What am I doing here?' The large, almost over-generous mouth split into a grin that showed white teeth. 'Don't tell me you've forgotten that we have a house here, right up on that cliff above you?'

Jane shook her head, trying to clear it from the mists of the past. Why was it that Miguel and his sister had always had the power to tie her up in verbal knots? 'You know I don't mean that!' she retaliated furiously. 'I mean what are you doing down in the port here and now?'

The black eyes narrowed into secret laughter. 'What a belligerent little thing you still are! I have to admit I was afraid you might have changed over the last—what is it? Five years?'

'You know damned well how long it is!' she hissed back at him. 'You never forget a thing, do you?'

'Not if it is important,' he agreed, still grinning at her before putting up one arm to get the waiter's attention. Jane seethed inwardly as the waiter responded to that arrogant summons with what she thought of as indecent haste.

She leant back and shut her eyes. She must, she must regain control of herself and not allow Miguel to continue to bait her. It was shattering to have to acknowledge to herself that his magnetic and commanding personality had become even more so in the intervening years.

Of course, he never had been a young girl's dream of a handsome hero; no Mel Gibson—his looks were far too forceful for that, the face dominated by his large nose and mouth, but once seen it was never forgotten. He wasn't enormously tall, and it would never be possible to describe him as elegant, but he had a raw power, a mesmeric effect on people that was nothing to do with his great wealth. He somehow seemed to diminish other men, as if once within his orbit they were reduced to the role of mere sycophants or people of no importance.

Jane felt crushed under the weight of his personality; she always had done. He was too rich, too powerful, and altogether too much for her. She had always tried to fight falling under his spell, and she wasn't about to change.

How was she to get away to meet Carlos? Their meeting would be doomed if this giant fly in the ointment persisted in hanging around her. A discreet look at her watch slightly reassured her. Surely there would be time to walk away before returning at the appointed time?

She opened her eyes suddenly to catch him looking at her with an expression she couldn't read, but before she had a chance to do more than draw her brows together his expression had changed back to the teasing one she was familiar with.

'Juanita tells me you have a holiday job out here as a cook?' he queried, and the look of doubt that crossed his face as he said that had her responding fiercely.

'Yes, I do and, what's more, it's going very well, thank you very much!'

'I suppose you're working for English people?' She should have ignored the disparaging note in his voice, but she told herself in mitigation that even a saint would have responded under that provocation.

'It wouldn't matter if they were French or Spanish, or Arab—they'd still be satisfied!' she answered through gritted teeth, and, deciding that she'd had enough, got up smartly to leave, just as the waiter appeared at his side with two coffees.

One hand shot out to circle her wrist. 'Sit down, Jane, I've ordered you another coffee.'

She looked at the powerful arm, the dark hairs alive with springing life, the gold Rolex, that only obvious outward symbol of his great wealth, and her mouth twisted in a sneer. Big grey eyes lifted to meet the dark ones, the scorn and distaste Jane was feeling all too obvious to the man who was watching her so closely.

'Let me go, Miguel. I'm not one of your bimbos, ready to do anything you want!'

His hand tightened its grip painfully, and something dangerous flashed in the depths of those dark eyes, reminding her of what had happened in the past between them. Scorn gave way to panic.

'Let me go! You've no right to keep me here against my will!' His fingers bit painfully into her soft skin.

'Don't be so melodramatic, and sit down...' He used his superior strength to force her to collapse back again into the chair, the iron of its back biting sharply into her spine.

'Let me go!' she still blazed at him.

'Not until you come to your senses and drink your coffee!'

'Not until? Have you gone mad, Miguel? There's nothing wrong with my senses! It's yourself you should be worrying about, not me!'

'Mad?' He turned the word around slowly. 'I suppose you could say so, but I am beginning to find it rather a pleasant state myself. Perhaps you too should try it?'

'Try what?' she demanded rudely. 'Try falling in with your wishes? You ought to have learned five years ago that there was little chance of my doing that!'

'You think so?' He gave a soft laugh. 'Just because I left you alone then, gave you a chance to grow up, it doesn't mean I've forgotten what I didn't take from you...'

Jane gave him her false smile, outrage at his words overcoming all caution. 'You left me alone?' She emphasised each word slowly, then she shook her head, her grey eyes never leaving his burning black ones. 'Is that what you think? I said no to you when I was seventeen, and, believe me, Miguel, the intervening years haven't changed me! You have to be sick if you can kid yourself any different... No means no in my book!'

'Then I shall just have to prove to you how wrong you are, won't I?' he answered smoothly. 'Now stop being so dramatic and drink your coffee. Carlos will wait for you.'

Jane, who had been on the point of sipping her coffee, nearly choked. 'You know I'm meeting Carlos today?' she demanded, the shock of hearing his name on Miguel's lips completely disarming her.

Miguel gave her the sort of look that people reserved for a slightly slow child. 'God knows why you're wasting your time on him, Jane. He's not the man for you, and I should have thought you'd have realised that by now.'

A great tide of colour flooded Jane's face. 'How dare you try to interfere in my life?' She picked up her undrunk coffee and flung it into his face.

He winced under the attack, but the black eyes still held hers in a grip of iron. 'Why won't you admit the truth?' he asked softly, then he let her go, turning away from her and pulling a handkerchief from his pocket to wipe the hot liquid from his face.

Jane was taking no second chances. She walked away quickly, her head held high. One question was pounding away inside her head. Why? Why wouldn't Miguel leave her alone? It was stupid to allow herself to think he was seriously interested in her—anyway, he was the last man she'd ever tangle with. It was maddening that he had the ability to infuriate her so much that she was betrayed into saying and doing things that her rational mind wouldn't consider for a minute. He had never asked for more than kisses from her, but that hadn't hidden the fact he had wanted a great deal more. As far as she was concerned, he'd behaved like an over-sexed brute, she told herself defiantly, and why he had to pick on her, when there seemed to be thousands of girls only too keen for his company, she couldn't imagine.

He always was contrary, she reminded herself bitterly, just like his sister! Tell them they could have something, and immediately they weren't interested, although they'd been moving heaven and earth for the favour a few minutes before. She sighed as she quickened her steps, heading for the jetty where Carlos kept the *Viviana*, but her joyful steps were slowed when she saw what was ahead of her.

Carlos and Juanita were part of a laughing crowd
of people, and it became clear to Jane, watching
from a distance, that there was no question of her
going out alone with Carlos today. She sighed. Well,
it had been her fault, hadn't it? She knew she should
never have let Juanita know of her plans for
Thursday.

'Willing to concede defeat in the first round?'
the hateful, teasing voice demanded from behind
her. She spun on her heel, leaving her expression
to say it all, not even bothering to waste her breath
on speech. A soft laugh, full of pleasure at her discomfort, had her mouth twisting maliciously.

'Why don't you go home and change? You look
a mess, birthday boy,' she sneered.

'Good idea. And why don't you come with me?
Unless——' Miguel jerked his head downwards
towards the noisy, chattering group on the jetty
'—you want to join that lot for the day?'

Jane was torn with furious indecision. Her immediate reaction of refusing Miguel's offer would
be rather like cutting her nose off to spite her face
if she was condemned to spend the day with the
load of chattering idiots waiting on the jetty. She
knew most of them, and knew she was of scant
interest to them, being just Juanita's little friend
from England and therefore of no importance in
their scheme of things.

She gave Miguel a considering look. 'I was going
to spend the day at sea . . .'

'Good idea!' he riposted. 'We'll go out in my
yacht instead.'

'Your yacht?' she queried.

'Yes, didn't you know I had one? The *Teresa* is waiting for me over there.' He gestured towards the marina proper, where Jane saw a graceful white yacht that looked twice as big as any other in the port.

'It just has to be that big one!' she told him scornfully, but even so she allowed him to take hold of her elbow as they walked away from Carlos, Juanita and her friends. 'Oughtn't I go and tell them I'm not coming?' she asked him, suddenly stopping in her tracks.

There was a quizzical expression on Miguel's face as he looked down at her. 'I shouldn't worry. He'll get the message when he hears he's been stood up for me!'

'Stood up? But you couldn't know I would... Oh!' Jane's expression of outrage said the rest. Arrogant man! How dared he persuade her to change her plans? She noticed the corners of his mouth beginning to twitch with amusement.

'I would have made a good general, wouldn't I? After all, they say the secret of military success is forward planning, and I'm quite good at that, wouldn't you say?'

She slowed down, then stopped to look at him. 'You have about as much finesse as a charging rhino! I don't like being mentally flattened and physically hijacked just because you want a change from all those brainless-looking idiots you normally run round with. So—thanks, but no, thanks! You can spend the rest of your day alone, or with some of your usual playmates——' she shrugged her shoulders carelessly '—but you aren't going to spend it with me!' She turned round and walked away, her body betraying her outrage in every step as she listened to his soft laughter.

'You ought to be flattered that I should want to spend it with you!'

'Oh, why?' She stopped to turn round and stare at him.

'Because I'd have thought that even you would have worked out by now that I'm one of the most eligible men in Europe! Girls go to extreme lengths to stay in my company!'

Jane shook her head at him. 'I can't believe what I've just heard! You're so arrogant, it isn't true. Anyway, I'd have thought you'd have learnt by now to be a little ashamed to be loved just for your money!'

'You think that's my only attraction?'

Jane longed to rub that smile off his face. 'Well, you'd hardly qualify as a model for Adonis, would you?' she retorted.

'So you haven't grown out of liking pretty boys, then? You should try falling for a man some time, darling. You might find it illuminating!'

'Miguel, just what is it with you?' Jane demanded. 'Why can't you let me alone?'

He laughed silently at her. 'You amuse me, the way you always respond to my teasing. I like to see how far I can go... But if your heart is set on having a good time with Carlos, then off you go, and don't blame me if it turns out to be a disappointing day!'

She was in such a temper, such a rage, that she didn't hear or see Carlos until he took hold of her arm.

'Hey! I wondered where you'd got to...' He gave her a sharp look. 'Listen—Juanita and a group of friends are trying to join us, but so far I've managed to put them off... Do you want to go out in a crowd, or just with me?' She thought he looked just a little unsure of her answer as she surreptitiously checked that Miguel was no longer around.

She tried to gather her tempestuous thoughts into some kind of order. 'You—you don't want to go out in a crowd?' she demanded, also a little uncertainly, finding it hard to believe.

Carlos's smile was warm, had gained in confidence. 'Oh, no... I think we'd have more fun alone together, don't you?'

Now this was an unmistakable invitation, and if she hadn't still been caught up in a reckless desire to put Miguel and his family in their place she would never have accepted quite so willingly.

'Of course we could!' she told him, but her rather forced enthusiasm rang distinctly false to her own ears, although Carlos looked delighted.

'I've told them we're going north, so we'll go south, shall we, down to Porto Cristo?' His voice was lowered as they made their way down to where the *Viviana* was moored. Jane smiled generally at the myriad greetings called out to her by Juanita's friends.

'Hi, Jane! Didn't I see you with Miguel just now?' his sister enquired blandly.

'Hi! Yes, you did.' Jane smiled at Juanita's obvious annoyance at her short answer.

'So what's the plan?' a lazy American voice enquired.

'We all meet for lunch in the yacht club at Puerto Pollenca!' Juanita announced loudly. 'OK, Jane?'

Jane smiled. 'I'm in Carlos's hands today, but it sounds fun, so why not?'

It seemed to her that Juanita gave a tiny sigh of relief before her familiar expression of bored superiority took over. Carlos didn't seem prepared to waste much time once the decision had been taken, and apart from refusing to take a couple with them, which Juanita tried to organise, soon they were on their way.

'I gather the weather forecast's good?' Jane shouted over the far from muted roar of the powerful engine as they swung wide out into the bay as if they were indeed going north. She had been extremely surprised to see Juanita down on the jetty this early in the morning, and it confirmed her suspicions that she really had to be interested in Carlos.

'Fantastic!' he responded with a smile. 'We're going to have to go quite away out to sea, but then we would anyway even if we intended to keep our rendezvous at Puerto Pollenca.' He gave her a grin. 'I haven't had such fun playing truant since I left school...'

'Don't you think Juanita and the others will be cross if we don't turn up?' she demanded slyly.

He shrugged. 'Why should she? There are always so many people around that girl that I can't believe she will seriously miss our company among so many.'

Aha! Jane thought. So that's the problem, is it? Maybe he is interested in her after all . . . Honesty, though, compelled her to explain the reasoning behind that crowd of ever-present people.

'It isn't her fault, you know,' she told him. 'Her parents insist that she never goes anywhere alone because of the threat of kidnapping. She has her own personal bodyguard and he has to be with her all the time, and I know the only way she feels she can lose him is in a crowd. It isn't exactly all fun being Juanita de Tarrago, you know.'

He shrugged again rather irritably. 'I suppose not . . . Even so, I still think she quite enjoys being surrounded by so many people.'

'Maybe it's her protection against feeling a little inadequate,' Jane answered quickly, surprising both herself and him.

'Hey, you really are her friend, aren't you?' Carlos took off his glasses to give her a serious, rather questing look before turning once more to scan the horizon.

Jane couldn't begin to explain why she felt she had to stick up for Juanita, who would certainly never return the compliment in a million years. 'It isn't easy being her friend. I mean, everyone always thinks I'm out for what I can get, and that makes me mad! Juanita as well . . . She's so used to that particular attitude in the people who surround her that she sometimes forgets I'm different.' She gave a big sigh. 'I don't really want to be her friend at all. I hate most of the people who hang around her, and I find anyone with that amount of money obscene!' She tried to laugh. 'You probably think I'm mad; most people seem to, at least those that hang around the Tarragos . . .'

'No,' Carlos answered. 'I can understand very well what you have just told me. I didn't know, though, that you are a friend of Miguel's.'

Jane stiffened in outrage. 'I am *not* a friend of Miguel's! He's the most irritating, bossy, arrogant man I've ever met in my life, quite apart from being over-sexed!'

Carlos grinned at her. 'I thought girls liked men to be over-sexed?'

'Depends on the man!' Jane answered, and he laughed, but she wasn't too sure about the sideways glances he kept giving her after that.

The *Viviana* was surging her way powerfully out to sea, her long creamy wake in startling contrast to the extreme blue of the sea, when Carlos started the gentle curving turn, taking them away from where Juanita and her companions expected them to head. Jane had relaxed once she'd got used to the heavy thumps of the hull on the swell of the waves, and started to work on her tan.

'You're sure you don't want to water-ski?' Carlos queried after an hour or so. 'You're beginning to look quite hot!'

Jane sat up. 'I'd simply love to!' She found it intensely exhilarating then to be towed mile after mile right out at sea, until the strain on her arms became too much, and she collapsed gracefully back into the water. She was revived by Carlos with a long, cool drink, and was lounging back in the seat, her face turned towards the sun, her eyes shut, when she became aware of trouble. The engine spluttered a few times, then died on them.

Carlos, his face perplexed, ran a series of checks. 'It shouldn't be possible, but I have a nasty feeling we have run out of fuel!' he told her, still with that puzzled frown on his face. 'I can't understand it. Tomás knew I was intending to take her out today for a long trip, and he told me he'd filled her up . . .' He looked down at Jane. 'You didn't smell any gasoline when you were being towed, did you?'

She shook her head. 'No, there was nothing that I was aware of at all. What do we do now, Carlos?'

He shrugged. 'There isn't a lot I can do, I'm afraid, except just sit and wait until someone sees us. I'm really sorry to have spoilt your day off, Jane!'

'But you haven't!' She gave him a smile. 'I've had a fantastic morning. So, OK, it's bad luck this has happened, but if you're sure we'll be picked up . . . ?'

'Yes, you don't need to worry about that! There are plenty of yachts about, quite apart from fishing boats . . . Someone'll come and see what we're up to soon.'

'It's a good thing you carry supplies around with you,' she teased, pointing at the two large cool-boxes that were full of the soft drinks she adored.

'Maybe it's a blocked fuel jet . . .' Carlos mused. 'But I don't think so. I think the tank is empty.'

Jane could see she wasn't going to get much of his attention until he'd worked out the problem. In some ways that pleased her. She'd had a nasty moment when she'd wondered just what he would suggest to pass the time, but for the moment anyway all his attention was centred on the *Viviana* and her inexplicable breakdown.

Just when her first suspicion that Miguel had something to do with this was a moot point whether it was before or after she'd first seen the graceful white yacht bearing down on them. Carlos— innocent fool!—was wholeheartedly pleased to see the *Teresa*, never for one minute thinking it was anything but the luckiest of coincidences, but Jane couldn't help remembering Miguel's earlier boast about being prepared. Although that's quite the wrong expression, she told herself, because there's no one less like a Boy Scout than Miguel de Tarrago! She also knew that, in this battle of wits, Miguel's deviousness would easily outclass Carlos's niceness.

Therefore she was totally unsurprised when the yacht, her sails temporarily lowered, dispatched a speedboat to their assistance. Since it had only a couple of crew members in it, but also several cans of fuel, Jane wondered if Carlos would swallow this seemingly heaven-sent help.

Her opinion of him sank even lower when he did, and he even agreed that it was sensible for Jane to transfer herself to the yacht as well, so that he and a crew member, and the cans of fuel, were left on the *Viviana* to sort out the problem. She tried to insist on staying, but Carlos, his mind so very obviously not on her, wouldn't hear of it.

'Jane, I'm sorry, but I couldn't ask you to stay here with me until we have sorted out the problem,' he told her earnestly. 'Anyway, you'll have much more fun on board the *Teresa*.'

She tried to stifle the feelings of incipient boredom that threatened to overwhelm her at the thought of having to spend the rest of the day with Miguel rather than him, and that infuriated her. 'But I want to stay with you, Carlos!' She almost stamped her foot in frustration at his inability to read her mind.

'Do you?' He gave her a narrow stare. 'Or is it that you don't want to spend the day with Miguel? I saw the two of you this morning. It looked to me as if you were prepared to go along with him at one stage until you changed your mind!'

His sudden attack of acuteness threw her completely off balance. Her cheeks became scarlet with embarrassment. 'No!' she exclaimed.

'Look!' He came close to her, and cupped her face in his hands. 'We can see each other this evening at the party, yes? Now my mind is all on another girl who is very dear to my heart—the *Viviana*! So go and have a good time with Miguel.

You're unlikely to find yourself alone with him, I assure you...' He smiled, then gave her a quick kiss on her cheek. 'Go now, before I change my mind!' There was little she could do in the face of such unexpected authority, so she smiled and accepted her fate with just the smallest of shrugs.

'I'm sorry your day has been spoiled,' Miguel greeted her.

'No, you're not! I think it ninety-nine per cent likely that you arranged it!' Jane's grey eyes were stormy.

'Temper, temper! Now why should you think that?' he demanded smoothly, his warm, suntanned body firmly placed strategically in front of her so that she couldn't pass him on *Teresa's* narrow deck without having to squeeze really close to him.

'Because you like to get your own way, and you're prepared to go to almost any lengths to get it!' she spat back at him.

He laughed. 'How well you know me! Come and meet my other guests.'

'Did you arrange for the *Viviana* to run out of fuel?' she demanded fiercely.

Two thick black brows rose and his mouth tilted into its usual teasing expression when he was talking to her. 'Now you really can't be naïve enough to expect me to answer that truthfully, can you?'

'Why not? You've never shown any inhibition about telling me things in the past!'

'And I can't recall any particular reluctance on your part to share my adventures, however vicariously!' he responded.

'This isn't the same thing at all!' she snapped.

'Isn't it? I think it is. The difference this time is that it is your plans that have been thwarted.'

'Nonsense! My plans indeed! I had none, except the wish to spend the day with Carlos—something perfectly normal and ordinary which you, with your sophisticated tastes, wouldn't begin to understand!' said Jane angrily.

'No? I hoped that's exactly what you would do, however, with me!'

'Then why is this yacht full of your friends if you wanted to be alone with me?' she demanded.

His eyes narrowed with laughter. 'As you chose to spend the day with Carlos, what was I to do? Sulk all by myself? No, you should know—none better in fact—that that has never been my style. So Bárbara and Mariana decided to take pity on me.'

It was Jane's turn to sulk. She knew she'd never get him to admit to her that he had anything to do with the breakdown, whether it was true or not. 'Well, you don't need my company, then, if you've got two women with you!' she retorted.

He gave a great sigh. 'Unfortunately I do, *querida*. You see, both Bárbara and Mariana happened to bring along their husbands.'

'Bad luck!' She wished he would move. She felt claustrophobic having him so close to her.

Without warning, almost as if he could read her mind, he pulled her against him, his strong arms holding her a prisoner against his maleness. 'You'll stop fighting me one day!' he told her, his black eyes still alight with wicked mischief.

Jane tried to wriggle free, until she realised that the movements of her body were exciting him. She caught her breath, aware that a strange and unaccustomed excitement gripped her also. Her body remained tense, still braced against his strength, but she was finding it harder to maintain her defiance as her grey eyes met the wicked black ones.

'I want to kiss you very badly, Jane, but this time I won't do it unless I have your permission.' His voice sounded low and deep, smooth and rich, like dark chocolate. One of his hands was very gently caressing the nape of her neck, sending delicious *frissons* up and down her spine. 'May I?' His head lowered over hers, and she found herself incapable of saying anything as his lips, oh, so gently, found hers, then later, with his tongue teasing their outline, she opened her mouth so that she too could savour and remember the heady sweetness of his kisses that, however hard she'd tried, she had never been able to forget.

A sudden lurch of the yacht, as she started to get under way, threw Jane, now unresisting, heavily against his body. A surge of heated excitement passed through her with all the speed of a flash-fire as she felt the pulsating heat in his groin. Alarm bells began to ring in her mind.

'No, no!' Frantically she turned her head away, trying to avoid his seeking lips, and he loosened his hold on her.

'Now what's the matter?' His voice, low and seductive, made the bells ring even louder in her ears.

'Miguel! Will you please leave me alone?' Seriously ruffled, Jane tried to calm her frazzled nerves.

'But why? Didn't you enjoy my kiss, little innocent?'

Jane tried furiously to stop the colour from flooding her cheeks, but it was no good—the tide of embarrassment was too fierce to be stemmed. He laughed at her discomfort.

'It isn't funny, Miguel!' she snapped.

'No, my darling, it isn't. It's quite painful for me as well, you know.' For the life of her she couldn't stop her eyes from sliding lower to see, with half-hidden excitement, the evidence of her power over him before rising again to meet his eyes. She had to fight him. He mustn't be allowed to win so easily all the time, and she'd do well to remember the expression 'practice makes perfect'. He'd certainly had a great deal of that.

'I'm sure you'll see to it that you won't have to suffer too long!' she told him scornfully, wanting to walk past him, yet not quite daring to do it. Luckily for her they were interrupted, and by a blonde girl of such spectacular looks that, quite without her knowing why, Jane's heart sank right down to her feet.

'Hi! So this is where you've been hiding, darling...'

'Mariana,' Carlos smiled, 'meet Jane. We were just on our way to join you all.' Feeling rather like a sparrow who had been mistakenly shut in a cage full of the most gorgeous love-birds, Jane smiled at the beautiful Mariana, and the equally beautiful Bába. Both girls were so much taller than her that she felt a freak, and she wasn't too surprised when neither of the husbands, after superficial assessing glances, bothered to waste too much time on her. After all, she was as out of her depth in this sort of company as a mongrel would be at Crufts.

But it seemed as if Miguel didn't share his friends' feelings. For whatever hidden reason he kept Jane close to his side, flattering her with extravagant compliments until even the others began to take serious notice and to treat her as someone of importance.

Jane, alternately shattered or beguiled by Miguel's blatant charm, found the whole afternoon stressful in the extreme. So OK, Miguel wanted to take her to bed. What was so terrible about that? She didn't have to say yes, did she? She could wish he'd stop making quite such a performance of it all, but surely she needn't feel quite so threatened by his slightly over-the-top tactics?

He became more and more outrageous, until she lost her temper with him. 'Will you leave me alone?' she howled at the top of her voice after he pretended to nibble her shoulder. His physical closeness was driving her mad as she strove to keep a distance between them. 'I am bloody well not going to end up one of your mistresses, so stop wasting your time!' She got up and stalked away below decks, desperate to get away from him and his teasing.

She was followed by Bába. 'Hey, did you mean that?' she queried. 'I mean no one, but *no one* turns down Miguel!'

'Then it's about time someone did!' Jane spat back. 'He's obviously had his own way for far too long...' The other girl was looking at her with frank curiosity.

'He's really set on taking you to bed, isn't he? I haven't seen him so hot for anyone since Donna May turned him down flat on the film set in L.A.'

'Oh?' Jane couldn't resist following it up. 'And did he succeed eventually?'

'Yeah, sure. She wasn't able to hang out against a mixed set of emeralds and diamonds to match her eyes ...'

Jane made a rude noise. 'Well, one thing's for sure! He won't be able to buy me that way, and he knows it!'

Bába looked at her with sudden and considerable respect.

'Good for you, honey! You hang on in there. Maybe you'll get really lucky and end up as his wife!'

CHAPTER FOUR

JANE dressed for the party almost deciding not to go. If Miguel persisted in singling her out in front of everybody then she would leave. She'd already threatened not to appear at all, but he'd just laughed in her face.

'You'll come, darling, you know you will!' He saw the fierce rejection of his words on her face. 'Oh, not for the reason that most other people do— I know that! But because you're loyal and a good friend to Juanita—better than she deserves, perhaps. I know how impossibly spoilt my sister is.'

'And she's not the only one who likes her own way!' she reminded him, her voice still sounding a little fierce.

'Now that's human nature, Jane. Everyone would like to have their own way!'

'But some more so than others!' she shot back at him.

'You should know,' he teased.

Just for the moment her temper hung in the balance, until a measure of common sense took over.

'I really don't know what it is exactly about you, Miguel, that irritates me so much!' she told him, her voice for once quiet and conversational when she was talking to him. 'But, whatever it is, I'm beginning to believe that I'm allergic to it. The cure for an allergy, you know, is pretty drastic. You cut it out of your life—forever!' Her voice rose on the last sentence.

Miguel shook his head. 'You're a little out of date, *querida*. The modern treatment is to desensitise yourself... and that means starting with a small amount put under the skin, just to check your reaction. Then——'

'Thank you very much, I know all about it!' she snapped. 'You're forgetting one vitally important factor. The person has to choose to undergo treatment. I understand most people tend not to do that. They prefer to avoid the irritant!'

He laughed heartily before picking up one of her hands, then kissing the back of it. 'You amuse me so much when you rise to my teasing. I keep thinking that you will learn not to one day, but somehow I now rather doubt it!'

She had been left once again without a word to say and a screaming urge to yell and stamp her feet like a child. Why did Miguel always have to get the better of her? And why couldn't he treat her with a little of that old-fashioned Spanish reserve and good manners that most of his grander friends treated their ladies with? Carlos, for instance, for all his come-hither looks, would never dream of upsetting her like this; he would be far too aware of her distress.

But was distress the right word? a nasty inner voice queried. Surely loss of temper would be more appropriate. Also, hadn't she already found Carlos a little boring, in spite of his good looks? She was, however, quite easily able to banish such renegade thoughts. Keeping a firm hold over herself, she sternly warned Miguel that she wasn't prepared to be made the cynosure of all eyes this evening just for his amusement. Whether he would respect her wishes, or treat her words as deliberate provocation for further attacks on her person, she would have to wait and see.

Luckily the party was informal, but she knew her outfit wouldn't count for much against most of the creations that would be worn there. It comprised a black silk and lace bustier, and leggings in swirling patterns of grey, silver and black, an outfit which showed off her slender figure to perfection even if it wasn't exactly in the couture class. She made her make-up a little more dramatic than usual, but there wasn't much she could do with her hair, and she certainly hadn't any intention of wearing any jewellery. She had already painted her finger and toenails a deep warm scarlet. Apart from the scarlet of her mouth they were the only touches of colour about her.

Juanita had insisted on sending a car for her at nine o'clock, which was ridiculously early for a party that didn't start till ten, but, in view of what had happened that morning, Jane didn't protest too much. She was bracing herself all the way over to the exotic modern summer home of the Tarragos for the wave of Juanita's fury to break over her because she and Carlos hadn't turned up at the yacht club for lunch.

At least she would be shut away in Juanita's suite of rooms watching her get ready, not open to Miguel's inspection while he was not being distracted by the guests.

She got the surprise of her life when she walked into Juanita's bedroom to find her already dressed in a simple demure dress of white lace.

'Good heavens! What's happened to the disco queen?' she couldn't help demanding. Juanita's taste in clothes had been fairly outrageous for a considerable number of years now. In fact they had been the centre of more family fights than anything else. Half the clothes in Jane's wardrobe had been given to her over the years by Juanita's mother in a desperate attempt to try and make her daughter conform to her own more conservative taste.

Jane had learnt fairly early on, though, not to consider them her own. Juanita would just come and help herself to whatever she wanted if she thought she could get away with wearing them away from her mother's eye. She had even warned Jane not to regard the outfits as her own. 'I don't want to see you wearing any of my clothes until I tell you you can!' she'd informed Jane when they were both fifteen.

Juanita's colour was a little heightened. 'I thought I'd try a change of image...'

'Well, you can certainly say that again!' Jane agreed, walking around her. 'Although it suits you, you know, in a funny sort of way...'

'What do you mean, "funny sort of way"?' Juanita demanded before sweeping over to sit down at her dressing-table to mess around with some loose strands of hair around her face.

Jane shrugged as she sat down on the large stool at the end of the bed. 'I don't know... Perhaps it makes you look older, more elegant. It's certainly a wonderful dress.'

Juanita heard the question. 'Alaia. Designed specially for me.'

'Well, there you go, then.' Jane shrugged again.

Juanita looked back at her from the big, silver-framed mirror. 'Was it your idea to go south today?' she asked suddenly.

'I'm afraid not. It was Carlos's decision to spend the day alone with me.'

'Was he cross when he broke down and you had to be rescued by Miguel?'

'No-o-o...' Jane answered slowly. 'I don't think so. Anyway, he said we'd have the evening together.'

A silver hairbrush went down with a crash, and Jane raised her eyebrows in pretended surprise at the petulant little display of temper. Feeling for once in control of the situation, she changed the subject.

'It all looks very pretty outside. How many people are coming?'

'About three hundred, I think,' answered Juanita.

'Some party, then!'

'I suppose so... How did you get on with Miguel?' Jane was aware of the quickening interest in Juanita's dark eyes, but refused to be intimidated.

'Just the same as usual!' she answered bitterly. 'He seems to find it immensely entertaining to provoke me into losing my temper!'

Juanita gave her a searching look. 'Do you really not fancy him at all?'

Jane felt the fierce colour flood her cheeks. 'How many times do I have to tell you that I don't, never have, as you put it, "fancied" your brother! He's the most irritating, overbearing man I've ever had the misfortune to meet, and it's about time you realised that fact!'

'OK, OK! No need to go over the top. I only wondered ... It seems you're fairly unique, then, because most girls seem to be mad about him!'

'They're probably only mad about the Tarrago fortune!' Jane finished waspishly.

'No, I don't think you're right. I know he's only my brother, but he's able to make most girls fall madly in love with him, and that isn't anything to do with our money!' said Juanita triumphantly.

'A fat lot you'd know about it!' Jane said rudely. 'You've never been able to tell who's a friend because they like you, or because of your money!'

'You're wrong, Jane. I've always known pretty quickly those who are out for what they can get.'

'You've been wrong about me enough times!'

'Oh, no, I haven't! I know when you get mad at me, but then, you see, I know you only stay my friend because at bottom you're sorry for me.'

The truth of Juanita's remarks hit Jane a shattering blow. 'Why—why, that's not true ...' she stuttered.

'Oh, yes, it is! Why don't you be honest for once? I know you don't like me very much; perhaps that's why I'm not always so nice to you.'

Jane was ashamed and also a little humbled at how well Juanita had seen into her character. 'OK, so you sometimes make me mad!' she agreed. 'But I'm only sorry for you because you're a Tarrago!'

Juanita looked at her intently. 'Do you mean that?'

'Of course, you gump!' Jane answered, using a word from their schooldays. 'I've always thought it must be ghastly having so much money. I mean, you can sometimes behave like a real spoilt cow, but underneath I've always been grateful it's not me in your position.'

Juanita turned right round to look at her, and for the first time gave her what looked like a real smile of true liking. 'I've always been jealous of you!' she admitted. 'People seemed to like you better than me, in spite of the money!'

'And I've always hated being treated just like your lady-in-waiting! Someone you can boss and bully into doing what you want!' Jane gave Juanita a sly look. 'And before you ask—no, I have not fallen in love with Carlos!'

Juanita's cheeks reddened. 'Ah! But can you say the same for him, I wonder?'

Jane grinned back at her. 'To be utterly crude, I'd be amazed to hear that his mind has risen much above my waist! You gave him a nasty shock by being my friend, and, although he's trying, I don't think he can quite recapture that first careless rapture when he thought I was just a little English tourist from the hotel who was out for a good time!'

'Seriously?' queried Juanita.

'Yes, seriously! But I did discover one thing about him. He hates you always being in a crowd...' Jane held up a hand to stop Juanita interrupting. 'Yes, I tried to explain to him about the body-guards and your parents, but that's your biggest turn-off as far as he's concerned.'

'I thought perhaps it was my clothes or something...'

Jane bounced up. 'Well, you look absolutely stunning tonight; worthy of being any man's wife, I promise!'

'You don't think I should change into something a bit more casual, like you?'

'Certainly not! Anyway, for starters this is your party, isn't it? So you might as well dress like a hostess for once.'

'You're beginning to sound like my mother!' Juanita complained.

'No, I'm not! There's no need to be a slave to the latest fashion unless one wants to be like the rest of the sheep who'll be coming tonight! You look beautiful, and if I have to flirt with your abominable brother I'll do it, just to make clear to Carlos that it's no go between us!'

'Would it really, truthfully, be such a strain?' Juanita demanded, with just a touch of a teasing smile lifting the ends of her lips.

Jane coloured. 'Oh, well, I don't know...' Then she straightened her shoulders. 'But he does make me mad!' she told his sister through gritted teeth.

'You look very sexy tonight, Jane!' Carlos's hold tightened as he tried to pull her closer to him on the dance-floor. 'Is this outfit for my benefit?'

'Sorry, 'fraid not!' she answered shortly. Carlos was being an absolute pain, she decided. After a promising start with Juanita just lately he had almost ignored her just to concentrate on Jane, even, she was to discover later, altering the place cards on the tables so that he was sitting next to her at dinner. Her initial politeness to him was beginning to wear very thin, particularly when she noticed her *entente* with Juanita was beginning to break up under his determined pursuit of her.

She began to be really worried about Juanita as she tried to keep an eye on her. Carlos having been greeted with evident delight by a petite brunette gave her her chance to slip away. She caught Juanita's eye, and the two girls managed to escape to her room.

'What is it? Have the two of you had a row?' Jane interrogated the unfriendly back as Juanita stood over by one of the long windows that looked down on to the terrace below them that was filled with people all having a good time. She received a shrug of the shoulders. 'He's found out that Miguel set him up with you this morning.'

'Oh, dear! But he doesn't really want me, I promise, Juanita. It's just his pride that's been hurt!'

'You could have fooled me!' the other girl answered indifferently. 'Anyway, if you really don't want him hanging around you, why don't you give him the push?'

'What the hell do you think I've been trying to do all evening? Don't you see? He's going to hang on to me just to prove to Miguel that his little plot failed!' Jane gave a big sigh. 'Why can't you understand? I don't much like the invidious position it puts me into either, I can assure you!'

'What can I do to help you?' Juanita demanded unhelpfully.

'You might at least tell Miguel what's happening—after all, it's mostly his fault, isn't it? If he hadn't tried to interfere then we wouldn't be in this muddle in the first place!'

Juanita turned to give Jane a sulky look. 'It was my idea . . . My idea that he should make a play for you, so that Carlos would know he wouldn't stand a chance with you.'

Jane stiffened. 'Your idea?' she echoed.

'Of course! I knew Miguel wouldn't bother with you unless I could give him a very good reason. He's actually very fond of me, and he knows I fancy Carlos!'

'Do you mean to tell me you set the whole thing up?'

Juanita shrugged again. 'Yes, of course. I knew it wouldn't worry you because you've always told me you couldn't stand Miguel . . . I told him that too, because he likes a challenge!' she finished a little smugly.

'So all he's been doing today is trying to clear the path for his little sister! Hell!' Jane exploded, finding it almost impossible to keep her indignation hidden. Juanita's words also hurt, but that she refused to acknowledge to herself.

'Come on, Jane! Why should it worry you? So, OK, it was a little unfair on you, but you've already told me that you don't care for Carlos or Miguel!'

'I don't like being used!' Jane snapped back.

'Well, perhaps it's better if you go home now. Shall I call a car for you?' asked Juanita.

'Go home before I've told your devious brother what I think of him? Never!'

'You do look cross!' Juanita appeared to have recovered somewhat. 'Come on, then! You'll need me if you're ever to separate him from Patricia!'

'Patricia?' Jane queried.

'Yes, the beautiful redhead. She has a hide thicker than an ox when she wants something, and she's unlikely to let go of my brother just for you!'

Jane followed Juanita towards the dance-floor that was set out near the edge of the great cliffs on which the house was built. The terrace here had been built in a great circle, with huge columns set in it at intervals. A more spectacular place for a party would be hard to imagine. A famous Mexican Tiajuana band were playing, the rhythm so easy and exciting to move to that Jane found it hard to keep her feet still.

'Be prepared to move in on him quickly!' Juanita warned her in a whisper. 'I won't be able to distract her for long!' Juanita had Patricia by the arm, and was pulling the reluctant redhead away from Miguel's side. Jane realised she would indeed have to move in smartly if others weren't to get there before her.

'I want to talk to you!' she whispered fiercely, as Miguel, resplendent in a white dinner-jacket, stood up from the table where he'd been sitting with a group of friends.

The black eyes narrowed into amusement as he took in the storm signals. 'Come and dance, Jane, then maybe people won't hear too many of the shouts over the music!'

'You're a louse, Miguel!' she snapped angrily.

'Louse? What is a louse?' The black brows had twitched with amusement.

'It's a nasty creepy-crawly!'

'Oh, dear!' Still the mouth twitched with hidden laughter. 'What have I to do to make reparation? I hope you have noticed that I have strictly left you alone this evening?'

Now Jane didn't know why she should be annoyed that he had, but she was. 'Yes, that's typical of you, isn't it? You've been crawling all over me like an attack of measles all day, yet come the evening, when there's a bit of competition, you don't even acknowledge that I exist except as a pawn in your little game with Juanita!'

He openly laughed at her. 'Oh, dear! And there I was thinking you'd be so pleased with me for leaving you alone!'

'I am!' she snapped back. 'But I don't like being mixed up in your little games without knowing about them!'

'What little games?' he queried.

'As if you didn't know!' she sneered. 'Look, most of the girls you run around with are probably thick, but I'm not! I've just got a good degree and I'm looking forward to starting my first job in September. You've made Carlos as mad as fire, and...' But she was destined not to finish. The sinuous redhead, quite ignoring her, danced between them, curling smooth brown freckled arms around Miguel's neck, proving that a good degree wasn't at all necessary to gaining and holding a man's attention. Miguel's wicked black eyes had narrowed further in amusement as he looked away from Patricia and took in the outrage on Jane's face. His mouth pursed as he blew her a kiss.

'Sorry, *querida*! But today is my birthday party, and I'm not sure I like being reminded that I am sometimes a bad boy...'

Jane was left standing, furious that she'd given him the power to humiliate her so desperately, and trying to resist the urge to push them both off the cliffs on to the rocks below.

She was claimed by Carlos, and she was still so mad at the way Miguel had allowed Patricia to cut in on them that she allowed him to appropriate her without any arguments. By the time she remembered that he too had a grievance this evening, it was too late. He was holding her close to him, trying to make it as publicly clear as possible that she was the girl for him and everybody had better remember it.

'Carlos, I know you're mad, but do you have to squeeze me quite so tight?' she protested.

'I'm sorry, Jane, I didn't realise you knew!'

'I know all right! Miguel is the most devious, impossible man I've ever met.'

'And I'm afraid his sister is the same... Somebody should teach them the lesson that it's unwise to interfere too much in other people's lives!'

'I quite agree that both of them need bringing down to earth—well, Miguel certainly more than his sister!'

'Juanita is too arrogant for her own good!' said Carlos. 'She has to learn that money cannot buy the important things in life——'

'I think she does know that,' Jane couldn't help interrupting.

'Then she has a very weird way of showing it. She as good as told me tonight that I was very lucky to have a chance of marrying her!'

'She didn't!' Jane was shocked and half disbelieving.

'Oh, it's true enough!' he told her bitterly. 'She knows I'm—well, fond of her, but I have never yet asked her to marry me, and after tonight I doubt I ever will!'

'I'm sure you must have misunderstood her.'

'Oh, no! She has put my love for her through enough hoops as it is. I do not wish to marry a woman with so much money—she should know that!'

'She probably does,' Jane soothed. 'Look, come and talk properly. It's impossible to be serious on the dance-floor!'

Carlos said gloomily, 'I don't want to be serious about anyone ever again—in fact, I won't be! You and I were going to have a good time today before the Tarragos decided to spoil it, so why don't we make up for lost time?'

It was at this point that Jane realised, albeit belatedly, that perhaps Carlos had been hitting the bottle.

It was difficult also to remember that she too was partly to blame for this mess. If she hadn't responded quite so enthusiastically—heavens, was it only this morning?—to his suggestion of them spending the day alone together, then perhaps he wouldn't still be so convinced that the green light was flashing for him.

She was conscious too of Miguel's glances at them both, and something in his expression made her raise her chin in defiance. He at least might be prepared to admire her from a distance this evening—if he did in fact admire her at all, which she was now beginning to doubt. He seemed to be perfectly happy to have Patricia glued to his side, a fact that perhaps was partly responsible for Jane's raised blood-pressure.

At last, after being driven half mad by Carlos's amorous advances, and his inability to take no for an answer as far as she was concerned, she escaped on the pretext of powdering her nose. Fed up with suffering from Juanita's reproachful glances, and Miguel's enigmatic ones, she used her expert knowledge of the house and grounds to escape and be alone.

There was a small paved garden at the back of the house, rather too near the busy kitchens for comfort, so for that reason little used by the family. This had long been a favourite retreat of Jane's when she wanted to be alone, and she sank down with relief on to the still warm stone of the wall that surrounded the central raised bed. The noise of the party, mingled with the clash of pans and all the extra staff in the nearby kitchens, masked any warning she might have had as someone approached her.

She was pulled to her feet, and before she had time to protest, or even see who it was, a mouth, both demanding and a little fierce, claimed her for its own. Just for a moment she'd been on the point of surrender, thinking only of one person who would ever have known that this was her private retreat.

But it had become clear that this was the wrong man. Two arms crushed her again painfully against the male body as once more that hard yet demanding mouth tried to force an entry into hers.

She resisted fiercely, knowing now who it was who had followed her. 'Let me go,' she threatened, 'or I'll scream!'

'Don't be such a spoil-sport, *querida*! Why change your mind so quickly? You seemed happy enough with my company this morning.' The slurred tones couldn't hide the sneer. 'Anyway, Miguel rejected you pretty publicly on the dance-floor just now, didn't he?' Carlos continued, his bitterness showing through.

'And I thought you were a gentleman!' she spat back. 'You know perfectly well that I don't want this . . .'

'So . . . I've been cut out by Miguel, have I? Well, this is one time when I'm not prepared to give in gracefully to the Tarragos. I've just about had them——' here he broke off to graphically draw a finger across his throat '—up to here!'

Once more his mouth claimed hers, half suffocating her, his superior strength forcing her to submit so that she began to feel faint in his arms. It was at this hopelessly inauspicious moment that Miguel, followed by Juanita, walked through into the tiny garden.

'Oh, how could you?' Juanita wailed, the pain in her voice making sure that Jane at least was brought back to reality. Carlos was still holding her in his arms and seemed intent on keeping her there. She shook her head free and took a great gasp of air, but this was all she was allowed, seemingly, before Carlos pulled her close to his chest, ignoring her somewhat feeble struggles to free herself.

'Why are you here, spying on me?' he demanded of Juanita. Jane heard the fierce pride, and with a sinking heart knew that something must indeed have gone terribly wrong between them earlier in the evening. She gave a violent, convulsive lurch, then managed to free herself, moving quickly away in case Carlos tried to entrap her once more.

Breathing heavily, she tried to wipe her mouth with trembling fingers, knowing that Carlos's assault would have smeared her scarlet lipstick. Carlos and Juanita were now both shouting at each other in Spanish. Jane looked up to find that Miguel was watching her with an expression of such distaste on his face that she was moved to protest. One hand was held toward him, the palm facing upwards in immemorial begging position, as she strove to regain some form of normalcy, but there seemed to be no life and no mercy in the dark eyes that continued to study her with what looked like remorseless dislike. Momentarily she shut her eyes, unable to face him, and when she opened them again he'd gone, sliding silently away into the night, leaving her feeling more bereft and helpless than she'd ever felt in her life before.

Carlos and Juanita were still fighting each other, so she managed to leave without either protagonist even noticing her departure. It wasn't difficult to get one of the staff to summon a taxi, but she was warned by a security guard that she would have to make her own way down to the main gates, because no one was allowed to enter the grounds.

It was with a feeling that somehow her life was now changed irrevocably that she collected her bag. A mirror told her its own shocking story. No wonder Miguel had walked away from her in disgust! Swollen lips, her skin liberally smeared with her own lipstick, her eyes ringed with black like a panda's... She bore all the marks of a girl who had been violently used, like some slut.

'Oh, God!' Just for a moment she shut her eyes in desperation, willing the tears not to fall, before with fierce energy she set about trying to put things to right. She had to get away from this scene of her humiliation, this fiasco, before anyone could try and stop her. She'd been used as a pawn just once too often in this chess game of life, and as before it was always the Tarragos' fault.

She'd been made to look a fool by Miguel, and Juanita had helped to set it all up. Jane owed her no more loyalty even if she did understand the desperation that had driven her. Juanita was a fool to have humiliated Carlos, because she doubted if he would ever forgive her. If he hadn't already been slightly drunk, she doubted if he would ever have even told her. Juanita had hurt and shocked him, and if the sight of him in her arms had even slightly helped to balance the books—well, Jane thought, it would have done her no harm to suffer a little herself.

As to the way Miguel had looked at her in the garden... Her heart began to swell with anguish. He'd had no right to look at her like that! It wasn't her fault she was being half crushed to death by a man who hardly knew what he was doing, was it? And it was partly his fault that the man was in that state in the first place! The righteous indignation began to take the place of the hurt. Who was he to query her behaviour? Particularly after the way he'd allowed that redhead to humiliate her. That had been cruel, and if she was honest with herself she had to admit that it surprised her, because, tease unmercifully as he did, never before had Miguel been deliberately cruel.

Angry tears at being so misjudged finally became the last straw. That's it! Jane told herself. Never again am I ever going to make the mistake of getting caught up with the Tarragos! They can play their sick games with others, but I'll be damned if they ever manage to catch me near them again!

She made her way down the brightly lit drive towards the main gates, aware that she had to be the first person to leave. Just before she got there, a figure detached itself from behind a tree.

'Jane, I don't want you to go yet—we have to talk.'

She looked back at Miguel without flinching, her grey eyes appearing to him as cold and bleak as a dawn in mid-winter.

'I have nothing whatever to say to you, and nothing you could say to me would be of any interest at all,' she told him, her voice cold.

'I was rather afraid you'd feel like that. By the way, I owe you an apology for that appalling display of bad manners on the dance-floor.'

'Too little, too late! If you found it so disgraceful, why didn't you do something about it at the time?' she retorted.

'Because she's the daughter of the president of——' He broke off. 'Well, let's just say I have a deal riding with that country that's worth a good few millions.'

'I would have thought you'd got quite enough of them already, but still...' Jane shrugged. 'I suppose I'm not too surprised that you put such a high value on money.'

'And I thought you might have learnt that having that much money brings enormous responsibilities with it!' he told her harshly.

'Responsibilities to make more?' she enquired sweetly. 'Anyway, I can't quite see what that has to do with the president of somewhere's daughter!'

'Stop being so deliberately obtuse! You know perfectly well that if that money is used properly it can bring prosperity and wealth to people who'd otherwise have not the slightest chance of bettering themselves!'

'No, and I didn't know that philanthropy had become the guiding light of the Tarrago family firm!' she told him fiercely. 'Now, birthday boy, why don't you go back and enjoy the rest of your party, and leave me to go home in peace?' He came to stand near her, and she drew back a step. 'If you lay a finger on me I'll scream!' she told him fiercely.

Just for a moment the ghost of humour played around his mouth. 'I'm sure you will!' he told her politely. 'All right! This obviously isn't the time and place to talk to you... The car is waiting to take you home.'

'I ordered a taxi!'

'And I cancelled the order, so either you walk with the car following you the whole way, or you're sensible and get in and let the chauffeur drive you home.'

'This is the very last time I'll allow any member of the Tarrago family ever to countermand any order I've given!' she told him through clenched teeth. 'And it's the last time I ever have anything to do with you and your family!' She swept past him and out into the road where the chauffeur was waiting to help her into the car. She didn't once look back, and there was a very thoughtful look on Miguel's face as he turned to walk slowly back up the drive towards the noise of the party.

CHAPTER FIVE

JANE had a hard time waking up the next day. The fiasco of yesterday had kept her awake with some pretty uncomfortable thoughts. It was Miguel's behaviour that she found the most strange. Why should he have bothered to leave the party to walk down to meet her at the entrance to the family house?

She had spent an extremely uneasy few hours remembering the expression on his face when he and Juanita had first found her. She could have sworn that as far as he was concerned she'd put up such a black that she would be the last thing on his mind for the rest of the evening. Yet he'd been lying in wait for her at possibly the only one place no one would think of looking for him—always supposing no one had seen him leave the house.

As she walked down to the village to buy fresh bread for breakfast, Jane found she was consumed after all with curiosity to know just what Miguel wanted to talk to her about. It was this ambivalence about her feelings that had kept her awake half the night.

Cold logic told her that the sensible course would be to have nothing more to do with the Tarragos, but logical thinking wasn't her strong suit, and undoubtedly Miguel's charismatic personality had had its effect on her.

It was difficult, but by the time breakfast was over, and she had done her day's shopping, she accepted that as far as the Tarragos were concerned she was outclassed, and always had been. Pride had ensured that for years she'd told herself they were no better than her, but in truth they were cleverer, and could run rings around her.

This was galling to accept, overturning as it did some of her most cherished long-held convictions. Secondly, she decided there could be no way of continuing whatever friendship there had been between them. They could shine on the European stage, stars by the very fact of their great wealth, and she would sink back happily into the obscurity that her very ordinary background demanded.

It was infuriating, therefore, to be caught on the hop by the phone, which rang, as far as she was concerned, far too early in the morning for it to be anyone dangerous, or so she thought.

'*Hola*!' she said.

'Good morning, Jane.' The familiar voice had her whole body stiffening in shock. 'I hope you didn't suffer too many bad dreams last night?'

'What do you want, Miguel?' she asked, hoping but doubting her voice sounded cold and distant, rather than warm and surprised.

'To arrange a meeting. You can't have forgotten I told you last night I wanted to talk to you?'

'I'm not interested in meeting or talking to you!'
Brave words; she hoped her courage would allow
her to live up to them.

'Jane, don't be tiresome! You're too fond of
making dramas, and what happened yesterday
would be better forgotten by all of us.'

'Really?' she answered flatly, the irritation she
could hear in his voice being enough to bolster up
her flagging convictions that she was doing the right
thing. 'Give me a good reason why, and I might
just accept it!' Her sarcastic response ought to make
him rethink his ideas. She was not going to be
trampled on again.

She heard him sigh. 'Very well, if it makes you
feel better to be difficult . . . Juanita and Carlos announced their engagement last night!'

There was a moment of complete silence, then
her resentment flared up. Why the hell did he have
to be right all the time?

'I hope he still wasn't too drunk to know what
he was doing!' she said spitefully.

'That's hardly a kind remark!' he reprimanded
her severely.

'And I didn't find being used and abused by
either of them particularly nice or kind either!'

'Look, both Juanita and Carlos know they owe
you a big apology,' Miguel told her.

'Big of them!' she snapped back. 'And what
about you? What about your part in this rather
sordid little drama? You set Carlos up yesterday,
but when I came to you for help in getting me out
of a situation that had gone horribly wrong you

just abandoned me on the dance-floor! I'm fed up
with your family just using me as a pawn that can
be pushed around, and I don't want to be mixed
up in any more of your plans!'

'It's a great pity that you still behave and think
like a child! I had hoped you'd have grown up sufficiently to look for the reasons behind certain of
my actions, but you're still too much at the mercy
of your emotions, aren't you?'

'If you say so!' Her voice, cold and sarcastic, hid
her pain. 'But at least I'm grateful that I'm still
human with all my faults, not a superman like you!
You've been living too long in the rarefied heights
of the super-rich—you've forgotten what it's like
for us more ordinary mortals, haven't you?'

'How dare you——?' She heard the molten lava
in his voice, and knew she had provoked him into
losing his formidable temper. Sheer bravado had
her interrupting,

'I dare! That got you on the raw because it's the
truth, isn't it? It's no good shouting at me, Miguel.
I'm not a member of your family, nor do I work
for you. I'm free to do my own thing, and that
means not having anything to do with the Tarragos
in the foreseeable future!' She banged the phone
down with satisfaction, but part of her was shaking
with reaction, and there were two bright patches of
colour on her cheeks.

Well, it hadn't taken Carlos long to change his
tune, had it? She wouldn't care to be engaged to a
man who was so blatantly chasing another woman
just hours before the announcement! She won-

dered just how quickly the engagement had occurred after that nasty little scene in the garden. The memory of Miguel's expression as he'd looked at her raised once more the compound mixture of fury and pain. She wrenched her mind away from him and tried to concentrate on Juanita and Carlos.

She found herself slicing tomatoes with such vigour that her fingers were in grave danger of suffering the same fate. Oh, well! Juanita had got what she wanted, and she hoped for Carlos's sake that he'd somehow put his foot down last night, otherwise his future life wouldn't be worth living.

She accepted a tearful phone call from Juanita early in the evening. 'Jane? Will you ever forgive us?' she wailed.

Having decided earlier in the day that nothing would induce her to forgive Juanita, Jane found her resolve weakened by the genuine remorse she detected in her voice. 'I expect so!' she answered drily. 'Anyway, many congratulations, and I hope you'll both be very, very happy together!'

'Oh, Jane!' She was surprised to hear a genuine choked sob. 'Miguel's given us such a row for what we did to you! He really tore a strip off Carlos...'

'Don't let it worry you, Juanita,' soothed Jane. 'It just means he's furious with me because I won't fall in with some plan he's concocting. We'll still be friends, won't we? But don't expect me to come and see you until your brother has left, will you?'

'I thought—we hoped... Mamá and Papá are here. We're having a celebration dinner.'

'No, ducky, haven't you forgotten I'm here to work?'

'I'll ask the Waterses . . .' Juanita went on excitedly.

'No. Miguel's already lost his temper with me once today, and I can't guarantee to behave in a civilised manner if I have to meet him again so soon!' Jane told her.

A weak giggle made her smile wryly at herself. 'He's certainly been in a temper all day!' Juanita agreed. 'Whatever did you say to him?'

'I just told him to stop behaving like God and come back to earth.'

There was an awe-struck silence, before Juanita giggled again. 'No wonder he's cross with you . . .'

'I'm equally angry with him!' Jane reminded her, before they rang off.

She quite expected to hear more from Miguel, but it seemed as if he wasn't too keen to go on banging his head against a brick wall, because he certainly made no more effort to contact her for the rest of her time in Mallorca. She had a charming letter of apology from Carlos for losing his head, blaming it on not being sure of Juanita's feelings for him, as well as for drowning his sorrows rather too heavily. Even Juanita appeared to have given up on her now there was someone else to fill her time, although they managed to speak every week; mainly the topics were plans for the forthcoming wedding, both girls fighting shy of any more intimate talk.

Miguel, for instance, was never mentioned at all, and Jane was too shy to enquire about him. Which all goes to show, she told herself, that he never was at all interested in me! Why this conclusion should plunge her into the deepest depression she refused to face, just as she told herself fiercely that she was right to have brushed him off so successfully.

She returned to England with such a sense of corroding disillusionment that it took all her relief at having a decent job to look forward to to make her life seem even halfway bearable.

Her mother and father, who lived in Devon, and were not the most introspective of parents, noticed that she was unusually quiet, and drew their own conclusions. Naturally they didn't enquire too deeply, but seemed to think it had something to do with Juanita's engagement to Carlos Vilafranca, in spite of her indignant denials.

'Darling,' her mother had said, 'tell me about Juanita and her fiancé.'

'Well, he's a nice man, I think, so she's been very lucky. It isn't easy for a girl in her position, you know...'

'I can imagine,' her mother agreed thoughtfully. 'Too much money can almost be as much of a curse as too little. We always felt very sorry for Juanita, but she coped very well on the whole, didn't she?'

Jane, aware that her mother thought Juanita a sweet girl, grinned. 'I suppose you could say so. For a girl who's been so spoilt, I suppose she's not too bad. Still, she certainly managed to upset Carlos the night they were engaged!'

'Oh, why, darling?'

Jane, cursing her unruly tongue, had to do some quick thinking. 'She'd been giving him a hard time, and I think she went a bit too far. He made it clear he'd had enough, so there was a row before they got back together.'

'And you got involved in that row!' her mother said with humour as she looked at Jane's shocked face. 'Oh, don't try to deny it, darling! I knew something had gone wrong. Did Carlos try to console himself with you?'

'Something like that!' Jane agreed, unwilling to elaborate any further.

'That must have been a difficult situation to cope with.'

'It was partly Juanita's fault. She tried to manipulate Carlos, with Miguel's help. She's very lucky he's forgiven her, in my opinion!'

'What's he like—Carlos?' her mother enquired.

'Tall, good-looking... He's a nice man, probably too nice for Juanita!' added Jane.

'What on earth do you mean?'

Jane had forgotten momentarily that she was speaking to her mother. 'Oh, Juanita's tough, you know! She can be quite a bully when she's set her heart on something.'

'Oh, dear! Well, I suppose some men like to be told what to do.'

'I don't think he does, so Juanita's going to have to be very careful. He's very Spanish, although his mother is English...'

'English?' her mother interjected with a smile. 'That's nice.'

'Don't be so insular!' her daughter laughed at her.

'Sorry, darling!' Her mother was immensely casual as she looked away and asked the next question. 'I don't suppose you met anyone interesting?'

Jane shook her head. 'Sorry, Mum!' She knew her mother longed for her to meet a nice man and settle down. A fleeting image of Miguel made her smile. What would her mother make of him? she wondered.

She'd been lucky enough, earlier that summer, to land a job with a small, go-ahead company that imported fruit and vegetables from Spain to England. They were contracted to supply only one large group of supermarkets, although they hoped to expand the business in the future. Her working knowledge of Spanish had helped her considerably in the interview, even though it hadn't been asked for in the job particulars.

A month later she had learned an enormous amount about the transport and marketing of Spanish vegetables. Most came into the country by road, where they ended up in depots before being distributed, but some soft fruit, like strawberries, were flown in. She learnt that most of the tomatoes came in from the Canaries, for instance, but she learnt also that cargo planes flew vegetables and fruit in from places as far away as Central America. In fact, never again would she be able to walk around the fruit and vegetables in a supermarket without remembering all she had learnt from Tom, who was her immediate boss.

After some initial strangeness, she seemed to have settled down quite well with him, although she was conscious that he and Mary, the secretary-receptionist, held her at a distance. Mike Ferrers, who was a little older than her, was obviously jealous of her degree, and deliberately kept out of her way, and none of the others were yet on such terms with her that she felt she could ask why and be sure of getting the true answer.

This was the only unsettling thing about her new job—this feeling that somehow she didn't really belong there with everyone else, that somehow she was an interloper. She tried to be friendly, and with Tom at times she thought she had succeeded, but the attitude of the others, from Richard Alston the managing director downwards, puzzled and defeated her.

She had left their small office one morning to check over a large consignment of oranges at a nearby depot when she discovered that she'd left behind some important documentation. She had walked back quietly into their small reception area to find that Mary wasn't there. Slightly surprised, she was heading for Tom's office when she heard her name mentioned by Richard Alston.

She stopped, and was about to announce herself, as she saw him, Mike and Mary through the half-open door to his office, where she'd first met everybody, when Mike interrupted him.

'How much longer is this farce going to go on?' he demanded. 'She's been foisted on us by someone we don't know, and heaven knows what for! She's had no business experience at all, and we're supposed to be creating a job for her! The only possible job she could do is mine, and I don't see why I have to step down because little Miss Pretty just happens to know the right people——'

'Mike, that's not quite fair!' Richard interrupted. 'There's never been any question of her taking over your job. We're supposed to be expanding!'

'Yes, but what possible use can she be? She doesn't know a thing about the fruit and veg market, transport, or selling!'

'That's something she's supposed to be learning,' Richard answered.

'Yes, but why? Why her, I mean? You know Peter Moore would have been the perfect choice to work with me, yet he didn't even get a look-in at that interview.'

'Well, he doesn't speak Spanish!' Richard was obviously trying to defuse the situation with a little humour.

'And what's the use of Spanish when we're supposed to be concentrating all our efforts here in the West Country?' Mike persisted.

'The big boss himself is coming over next week. If you feel so strongly, why don't you ask him yourself?' Richard riposted.

'I will! It's not as though I've really got anything against the girl—she seems pleasant enough, but I can't understand why she should have been chosen for a potential job which we all know would be far better done by——' The sudden scraping of a chair reminded Jane where she was. Without wasting any more time she was out of the office and walking blindly towards her small car.

She got into it, but made no attempt to start it; she was too shocked for that. Her thoughts tumbled through her brain in a hopeless jumble. Miguel couldn't have done this... Why she was so certain this had something to do with him she was never able to say afterwards, but she was. He'd engineered this whole job, just to get her working for him, and she'd been naïve and stupid enough to think she'd achieved it all by herself.

Why? She thumped the steering-wheel in exasperation. Was it a disinterested desire to help her find her feet in a business venture, or something more sinister? Out of the corner of her eye she saw Mike Ferrers walk out into the car park and do a double-take when he saw her car there.

Pride ensured that he wouldn't be the one to find her thrown off balance by what she'd just overheard. She opened the door and got out, giving him just a cool smile before walking past him.

'Hi! I thought you'd gone for the day.' Mary's slightly breathless greeting, as she came out of Richard Alston's office, showed how disconcerted she was at the sight of her.

Without stopping Jane walked past. 'I left some papers behind...' She noticed with a sour internal smile of amusement that Mary looked distinctly edgy, as if she wasn't quite sure how long Jane had been around, and whether she could have over-heard that indiscreet conversation between Mike and Richard. Let her sweat, she thought, as she bundled her missing file into her briefcase, before walking quickly out of the office she shared with Tom.

'Jane!' Mary began, but Jane ignored her.

'Sorry, can't wait—I'm late!' She continued walking, leaving Mary standing with her mouth half open. She found Mike waiting for her by her car, but her sudden belligerence gave her the courage to cope with him. There was a slightly worried smile in his eyes as he opened the door for her. She al-lowed her brows to rise in surprise.

'Had a change of heart, Mike?' The smile on her lips didn't meet her eyes as she threw in the briefcase. 'Sorry I haven't got time to re-ciprocate—I'm late!' She got in, and shut the door in his face, trying not to laugh at the comical ex-pression of dismay as she drove away. A steely de-termination began to grow in her, at once familiar and exciting. She'd show them! They might wonder why she'd got the job in the first place, but she'd soon show everybody that she was more than capable of making a place for herself.

She arrived at the depot to find Tom waiting for her, a worried frown on his face. 'There's been a right old mix-up, Jane, and they won't take the oranges! God knows how it happened, but I think the paperwork's gone a bit wrong at our end somehow. I think young Mike's to blame. But that doesn't solve the problem of a lorry off the ferry today fully laden!'

Jane bit her lip. 'It seems as if we'll have to try and find them another home, then, won't we? And quickly at that!' She frowned in concentration. 'Tom, let's see if we can solve this problem ourselves, right here and now.'

'Listen, love! I've got to report to Richard—he's our boss!'

'I know, but not quite yet. I've had an idea!' Quickly Jane outlined her plans.

'I don't know . . .' Tom was cautious. 'It's a good idea, I grant you that.' He looked at her with dawning respect in his eyes. 'And it could be the start of something new for us . . .'

'Look—it's about time I justified my position in the company. I know the rest of you resent me for some reason, so please let me have this chance to do something about it,' begged Jane.

Tom's cheeks deepened a little in colour. 'I'm sorry! Maybe we have been a little too quick to make up our minds about you.'

She smiled. 'I don't suppose it was all your fault. Anyway, it doesn't matter now. Let's try and see if we have even a ghost of a chance of saving these oranges from the city dump and the company from a loss!'

'Well done, Jane!' Richard Alston gave her a genuine smile later that day. 'I see you've certainly done your research pretty thoroughly on all the outlets available to us.'

'We didn't make that much money from the deal, but at least we didn't lose any, and maybe it won't be a one-off deal with the County Caterers!' said Jane.

'You've certainly worked very hard.'

'It wasn't just me—it was Tom as well!' she protested.

'Tom told me that all the ideas came from you. Mike Ferrers has a great deal to thank you for. If that deal had gone down, he could have lost his job, because it was sheer carelessness on his part.'

'Oh, well...' she shrugged, a little uncomfortably '...this is too small a company to apportion blame. We all stand and fall together, and most people make mistakes at one time or another in their lives.'

'That's very generous of you, considering the circumstances...'

She stopped him with a look, knowing that some things were better left unsaid if they were all to go on working together. 'I enjoy learning about the work. It's a very interesting and challenging job to try and build more than a toehold in this business!'

That was the truth, she told herself; it was surprisingly interesting learning about new things, and it was exciting to be part of a small group of people who intended to go places as fast as possible. Maybe she lacked the killer instinct that would take her to the top by not trying to kick Mike out and take his place, but she was honest enough to know that she couldn't do his day-to-day job as well.

Mike came to find her just as she was about to leave for home. There was a wary, half-resentful expression on his face. 'I gather I owe you a vote of thanks——' he began pompously.

'Well, as you're clearly about to bust a gut giving it to me, I shouldn't bother!' she interrupted, laughing at his affronted face. 'Anyway, I hope you'd just do the same for me if I made a mistake some time?' This at least forced a decent reaction out of him.

'Jane, I'm sorry I haven't always been quite fair as far as you were concerned...' he began, but she wasn't having any.

'Look, Mike, just forget it, will you? There's no point in looking back, only forward, OK?'

'OK...' he repeated reluctantly. 'If that's what you want!'

'That's exactly what I want! So why don't we get the others and go and celebrate with a drink in the Dog and Donkey over the road?'

'Sounds like another of your good ideas!' This time Jane got a reluctant grin. For the first time that evening she felt she had become an accepted part of the small group of people, and she smiled to herself, pleased with this, her first personal victory. Mike's mistake was forgotten as they all congratulated themselves on overcoming their first major set-back. All her other thoughts about Miguel were fiercely battened down, waiting only until she was alone before being taken out and looked at while she was undisturbed.

It wasn't until she got home that she was really free to think about the implications of staying with the company, and Miguel's connections with it, but fate was to intervene even then.

'Darling, Juanita called today!' her mother told her, her face alight with happiness as her daughter wandered into the kitchen. 'She absolutely insists that you be chief bridesmaid at her wedding!'

'Oh, no, Mum! I'd hate it... I only like to see children doing that, not adults!'

'She said you'd be difficult,' her mother said complacently, 'but I promised her that as one of her oldest friends you wouldn't let her down.' She saw her daughter's face, and her happiness faded away as lines of worry etched themselves on her forehead. 'Darling, whatever's the matter? Is it something to do with this man Carlos Juanita's marrying? I don't like to interfere, but is he the trouble?'

Jane tried to keep her own expression non-committal. How could she possibly explain her reasons to her mother? Neither of her parents would begin to understand why she felt so threatened by the Tarragos. Even if she told them her suspicions about her job, they'd just think how kind and what good friends the family had been to her to give her such an opportunity. 'No, Mum, it's nothing to do with Carlos Vilafranca, I promise you!'

'Then why, darling? I know you think I'm an idiot most of the time, but we could see you were unhappy when you came back from Mallorca.'

'It isn't something I can talk about!' Jane left the kitchen in a hurry to find sanctuary in her own bedroom. There she had to face up to the painful fact that what she'd just told her mother was the literal truth. True, because in spite of every good reason she could think of to the contrary, she'd committed the gravest folly of her life. She'd fallen in love with Miguel de Tarragos; joined the trail of broken hearts that lay in his wake, because she knew very well he was not interested in his sister's little schoolfriend.

He might fancy her—oh, yes!—but she rather doubted if he even knew the meaning of the word love, except in its most superficial state: desire. He could probably have any available woman in Europe if he put his mind to it, and she guessed she would rate pretty low on any list compiled of possible future wives.

He had teased her unmercifully over all the years they'd known each other, but he'd also lit a fire within her that had smouldered on unknown, until with appalling timing it had chosen to burst into a blaze of passionate awakening.

That summer when she was seventeen—that had been the start of it all between them. She began to relive those memories she'd so fiercely tried to re-press. The way he'd looked at her, seeming to be aware of her innermost thoughts. The hot pleasure she'd felt in his presence had been intoxicating as well as a little frightening. Her lack of experience over sex hadn't helped her confidence either. She'd had lots of kisses, but somehow she'd never been

tempted to take things further; but with Miguel . . .
He stirred her blood, woke her up and made her
aware of her body, of possibilities that previously
she had barely considered.

She'd known he would never be contented with
just kisses; that, if she gave in to him, she would
have to be prepared to go all the way because to do
anything else would be unthinkable. It had been a
heady experience, to feel her power over him, but
she'd always been aware she was walking on a
tightrope.

There was that time she'd gone too far, been too
provocative as she'd tried to assess exactly how
powerful an effect she had on him. She'd been
teasing him about one of his friends, a very pretty
blonde girl from Italy who had returned home
rather quicker than had been planned.

'Poor Giulia! She's really going to miss you . . .'
Jane had told him as he lay near her on one of the
sun-loungers up on the terrace near the house.
There had been no reaction, so she had half sat up,
deliberately trying to make herself look sexy as she
faced him. 'She seemed to think,' she continued,
'that without her you'd need to find someone else
to be your playmate.' Still there had been no reaction. 'She warned me to be careful not to stay
alone with you!' she finished with an artificial
shudder.

One eye had opened and surveyed her. 'Why,
Jane, it's certainly unusual for you to take such an
interest—such a close interest, I should say—in my

affairs. Are you feeling a little inadequate because so far you've been quite safe from my attentions?'

Colour flooded her face, and she lifted her hand to take a wild swipe at him. There was a brief, electric silence before he moved as quickly as a cat, pulling her over one shoulder. 'I think there's only one cure for your overheated imagination, my pet . . .'

Furious, she pummelled his back. 'Put me down!' she shrieked.

'All in good time, sweetheart.' He began to run, ignoring her protests, until he stopped suddenly. She turned her head and saw where they were.

'Oh, no! You wouldn't dare . . . Miguel, I've just had my hair done for the party tonight!' she wailed.

'I dare!' he told her softly, then he lifted her down into his arms and began to walk forward slowly towards the edge of the swimming-pool. Helpless in his arms, Jane became all too conscious of his strength and the slow, regular beat of his heart in his powerful chest. She veiled her eyes from the dancing brown ones so close to hers, but her muscles had tightened in anticipation. He bent his head and for a moment, a brief, endlessly disturbing moment, she felt his mouth possess hers. As she melted against him, she felt his muscles tense, then she was in the air, a confused tangle of legs, arms and emotions as the shimmering blue waters closed over her in shocking reality.

There had been other occasions, but never again had she dared to push her luck quite so blatantly. He'd shown her then that he was in control, and

of course she'd resented it as one more example of
his bossy control of her.

He'd found her in the little garden behind the
kitchens after she'd escaped one of Juanita's French
boyfriends who had seemed keen on promoting an
entente cordiale between them whenever Juanita
wasn't around. She had been sitting on the warm
stone of the central raised bed, her arms clasping
her knees, oblivious to everything except her own
hurt feelings at being chased by Pierre. It was her
pride really that was dented, but still it hadn't been
much fun trying to keep away from him, and ignore
Juanita's jealous possessiveness as far as he was
concerned. She knew Juanita was suspicious of her,
and was venting her own unhappiness on her friend.

The first she knew about not being alone any
more was when he came to sit opposite her.

'Seeking sanctuary, *querida*?' Miguel's smile was
soft, and just for once there was no sign of his usual
teasing malice being directed at her, so she relaxed
and smiled back quite naturally.

'You could say that,' she agreed.

'Why do you always come here?'

'Because it's so near the kitchens, no one ever,
apart from the gardeners, comes into it except me!'

'Is that why you like it?' She looked up, but
wasn't prepared to meet his eyes.

'I suppose so... Don't tell Juanita, will you?'
she finished with some urgency.

'No, I won't tell my sister. You come here quite
often, don't you?'

She shrugged her shoulders, before getting up and stretching. 'Not that often. It depends . . .'

'Depends on how difficult life is out there with all Juanita's friends?' he demanded, standing up to move close to her.

'I suppose so . . . Miguel, I really hate it when Pierre tries to make up to me on the sly. It's sort of degrading that he thinks I'm even interested . . .'

'Poor little one.' His voice sounded low and gentle. 'Complain to Papá—he'll soon send him packing!'

'And then I'd have your sister complaining to me for the rest of the holiday!' she riposted, trying to control her suddenly shallow breathing as he took her gently in his arms. It seemed so inevitable, so right, when his lips claimed hers, that first touch a gentle exploration, until they had both exploded, with uncontrollable passion, into a fever of touching, of holding . . .

He had spun her out to the stars with that first real kiss, and she'd responded with such real abandon that she'd felt him trembling with need as he'd pressed her young body close to his. It had been wonderful but somehow frightening for Jane to see for the first time a powerful man almost helpless in the grip of his desire for her.

She had looked back on that kiss and her feelings so many times over the past five years, and latterly always with regret, even if she had refused to admit it to herself. Now the wheel had come full circle, and the biter was well and truly bit.

How could she go back to Spain knowing this, yet still keep her sanity?

How was she to refuse? She wasn't strong enough to fight her own family as well as his, and she knew perfectly well from the past that if Juanita had set her heart on something then life would be hell until she got her own way. She dropped her head in her hands as she realised the appalling inevitability of it all. She felt like Napoleon at Waterloo—crushing defeat stared her in the face, but somehow she must try to gain something, at least her self-respect. To leave Miguel in such absolute control of her life was obscene. She would have to give up her job.

CHAPTER SIX

IT WASN'T easy for Jane to walk in the next morning and hand in her notice. To start with, Richard Alston refused to accept it, but when he realised her mind was made up his shoulders slumped.

'So you did hear us talking yesterday. Mary thought someone was outside listening.'

'Does it matter?' Jane enquired gently. He looked up to meet her eyes.

'Quite honestly, I sometimes wonder if the whole thing would ever have been started if it weren't for you!'

Jane was startled. 'Nonsense! You have to be exaggerating . . .'

'Well, I don't give much for our future if you walk out on us now!' Richard asserted.

She sat opposite him biting her lip, wondering how much she could believe. 'Surely you're doing well enough to stand on your own?'

He shook his head. 'Not yet . . . Give us a few more good contracts, then maybe we'll be safe, but we need more time to set them up.'

She stood up, unable to sit still. 'Oh, hell!' She swung round to face him. 'Do you realise I hadn't a clue until yesterday? Oh, I knew none of you liked me much, but I didn't know why! If I stay, I'll be in an impossible position—can you see that?'

121

'Which is worse—you being put in an "impossible position" or most of the others losing their jobs? Because quite frankly that's what it comes down to, you know.' He stood up. 'Look, I hate to beg, but I think we could make something of this whole thing. It was my idea in the first place— that's why I'm so keen to see it work. You believe in it as well, don't you?'

She shrugged helplessly. 'Yes, I do, for what it's worth.'

'It was the only way I could get started... I needed his help, both in Spain and over here. He's a shrewd devil; nothing much gets past him, does it?' Jane shook her head ruefully, knowing that even now neither of them was quite prepared to actually say his name. 'He agreed to back me on the understanding that I took you on, and made it appear you got the job on merit. Actually he did tell me you were quite bright enough to be an asset to me...' he shot her a quick look '...and he was quite right, as I learnt yesterday!'

'He isn't the sort of man who'd pull the plug on you now!' Jane told him vehemently. 'He believes in helping people to help themselves!'

'Maybe... but I'm not prepared to take a chance on it. Please, Jane, if you can't make it six months, make it three! Give us a chance to really get on our feet. It won't take long for us to know if we're going to make it. The competition's fierce, but with his backing...'

Slowly, reluctantly, Jane knew she would have to agree to Richard's demands, but there was one proviso she intended to make. 'OK, Richard, if you insist! But——' she held up one finger '—try to keep him out of my hair, will you? We fight cat and dog whenever we meet.'

He looked shocked. 'You fight? But that's not... I mean...'

'Forget it! You wouldn't understand even if I explained it to you. I don't even understand myself...' she finished a little sadly. She looked up, her eyes narrowed as she saw his expression. 'No, I am not his mistress and never have been!' she exploded, her eyes still full of furious resentment at his obvious disbelief. She thought of something else that it would be better to clear direct with him before he got any more wrong ideas. 'I'm warning you in advance that you'll have to let me go to Madrid for his sister's wedding, because I'm going to be a bridesmaid!' she finished defiantly.

Once Richard understood the implications behind her remark he couldn't stop a smile from spreading completely over his face. He came over to shake her hand. 'Jane, I'm sure you'll not regret this decision. Now, let's get everyone in here. We've got to plan a campaign to safeguard our future, and we haven't got much time to do it in!'

Miguel was supposed to be coming over the following week, Richard warned her, but surprisingly he did not turn up in the office, and if he was in contact with Richard, then he was playing his cards very close to his chest, because Richard didn't mention him at all to her. Jane had almost decided that he'd changed his plans when she got a call from him one evening at home.

'Jane? Hi! How are you?'

She noticed that he arrogantly hadn't bothered to announce who he was, just expecting her to recognise instantly that piercingly familiar voice. Well, two could play at that game!

'Who is it?' she demanded in a cool voice, but her little ploy was doomed to failure as a lazy laugh answered her.

'You know perfectly well who it is, *querida*!' Her heart was beginning to beat uncomfortably fast in her chest, but she knew she must still try to fight this monster who seemed determined to try to take control of her life.

'I thought I told you to leave me alone!' She tried to fight her feelings of panic. How could she stop herself betraying her secret if they met? He'd always seemed to have an uncanny ability to read her mind.

'Come and have dinner with me tomorrow night and tell me again,' he demanded outrageously. 'Anyway, we still have something to talk about, don't we?'

'We do?' she enquired faintly; her ability to stop him doing whatever he wanted as far as she was concerned was fast receding into the distance.

'We do!' he echoed firmly. 'How's the job going?' That brought her back to her senses. Hypocrite! she thought.

'Fine! I'm enjoying it very much.'

'Good. Then you can tell me all about it to-morrow night. I'll come and pick you up at your parents' house at seven-thirty. OK?'

'OK. Miguel?'

'Yes?'

'What are you doing over here in the West Country?'

'I've come to see you, of course!' he told her, then laughed softly at her inability to answer. 'Until tomorrow, then!' The phone went dead under her hand. Well, it looked as if Richard hadn't betrayed to him the fact that she knew the truth about her job either way, though she couldn't stop her heart from beating a mad tattoo of excitement at the thought of being with him again.

When she told her mother that Miguel was in the West Country and was going to take her out to dinner, she noticed the sudden arrested expression in the older woman's eyes, and just hoped she wouldn't be too embarrassing when he arrived to collect her.

'Mummy, will you kindly remember that as far as I'm concerned he's just Juanita's brother, and, even more important, I'm just his sister's little friend?'

'Yes, dear... But it's very kind of him to come all this way to see you.'

'He's probably just got a message from Juanita to twist my arm about being her bridesmaid, and of course he hasn't come all this way to see me! I imagine he's got business contacts somewhere near by.'

'Why, he might know the Spanish half of your company, darling! You must ask him...'

'Yes, Mother.' Jane hoped her mother would never guess just how right she was, and was pleased that some chore in the kitchen soon diverted her attention to the more important matter of dinner.

Jane was ready early quite deliberately; she didn't want him exposed to any more of her parents' company than she could politely get away with, and for once she was pleased that he didn't seem to want to spend any more time with them than his innate good manners demanded either.

'You look very pretty. Feminine but fragile!' he told her when he had got her alone. 'Mini-skirts suit you because you have very good legs.' He was formally dressed in a dark blue suit and a heavy cream shirt but with a rather flamboyant tie. He looked dynamic and surprisingly elegant, which she had never before considered possible, with his heavily forceful body.

'I'm not really tall enough——' she began, but he interrupted.

'Why on earth do you always try to run yourself down? It isn't a question of height, but of proportion. You might think of yourself as small, but you're perfectly proportioned, so your lack of height doesn't matter. In fact, you might say it makes you even more attractive!'

'Well, thanks! But I'd rather be taller!'

'Still contrary, I see,' he drawled.

'Only with you!' she snapped back. 'No one else thinks so!'

'Stop fighting me, Jane! Don't you realise yet why you want to do that all the time?'

It was difficult for her to hide the wave of colour that swept her face, and he laughed gently at her discomfort. 'I see you do understand!'

'I don't know what you're talking about!' Jane tried to sit up a little straighter, but Miguel's car, a Porsche, didn't seem designed for anything quite so unromantic; perversely the soft leather seats seemed intent on keeping her feeling laid back and relaxed. 'Where on earth did you get this car?' she demanded crossly, grateful for something on which to vent her irritation, which she was fighting to keep alive to stop herself being overcome by his closeness.

'I hired it. Don't you like it?'

'It's all right, I suppose, if you like this sort of thing, but you'll find that once you get on the motorway the police won't leave you alone for a minute!'

'I agree that it's not the attention of the British police I'm seeking at the moment,' he replied meekly. But Jane was not prepared to follow up that obvious lead, knowing quite well that it could have dangerous consequences.

'Where are we having dinner?' she asked.

'It's very small—I don't think you'd know it.'

'I know most of the places around here,' she told him, surprised at his unforthcoming answer.

'You won't know this,' he told her confidently. 'It's only just opened.'

'I bet I do! Why, you're not taking us to the Screeching Parrot, are you? It's awful!' she protested.

'No, we're not going there... What a dreadful name—is it a restaurant?'

'Not really, although there's a bar with snacks. It's more of a disco!'

'Thank God I've never heard of it!' The car swung round into a narrow lane, but there were no signposts and Jane couldn't see where they were heading, although she kept peering hopefully out of the windows. 'Nearly there!' Miguel told her.

'But we're heading up on to the Moor!' Jane protested. 'There isn't anywhere to eat within miles of this place!'

'Trust me.' The car was again turned carefully into a tiny lane that had sunk so deep that it looked as if the hedges were almost due to meet overhead, and the wild flowers whipped against the paintwork.

They pulled up in front of a long, low thatched cottage that was picturesque in the extreme. A yew tree in front had been clipped into the shape of a bird, and the tiny front garden was paved, but with a profusion of late summer flowers straggling over untidily from narrow beds that surrounded it. Two old-fashioned lanterns lit up the front porch, throwing their light out into the gathering dusk.

'Out you get!' Miguel said cheerfully, leaning across her to open the door, and she inhaled his heady perfume of sweet-smelling skin, and the tang of a faintly lemony aftershave, with all the discreet fervour of a secret addict.

'This isn't a restaurant!' she accused him, as she tried to force her drugged senses to behave normally.

'No, it isn't!' He grinned. 'I've brought Jorge and Carmen over to look after me. I've rented this cottage for a month.'

'A month?' She turned to look at him in wide-eyed astonishment. 'What on earth made you do that? You'll be bored stupid here in half that time!'

'I don't think so!' Jane felt him withdraw a little from her, as if mentally he'd distanced himself from his surroundings, and a faint chill settled on her shoulders, making her give a little shiver. It was this small movement of hers that seemed to bring him back to the present. He opened his door and got out. 'Come on in. There's no point in sitting out here getting cold,' he said.

She was able to get out of the car and walk into the cottage without any trouble because she was too busy trying to work out just exactly what it was Miguel had on his mind that could possibly entail renting a cottage for a whole month in the middle of nowhere. Well, nowhere, she qualified to herself, to him. He wasn't even particularly near an international airport, for heaven's sake; he'd go mad in a couple of days!

She greeted Jorge with a smile of distracted sweetness in the tiny hall, but she was too busy with her own thoughts to appreciate his smiling welcome as much as she should. What was Miguel up to? For a man with his almost manic energy this had to be craziness!

'Champagne, *querida*?' Jorge was standing by his master's side with a bottle.

'Yes, please, that'd be lovely... I wish you'd stop calling me darling,' she protested.

'But why should I?' Miguel laughed at her, as he watched Jorge hand her a narrow glass full of the sparkling glowing liquid. 'I think of you as a darling...' He took a glass himself, then raised it to her. 'To our better understanding of each other!'

Jane couldn't help her brows drawing together in a puzzled frown as she tried to work out any hidden meanings behind the inoffensive words. She had nothing against them precisely—in fact a better understanding between them ought to be a good thing; but...

Miguel raised his eyebrows. 'You don't think that an appropriate toast?'

She was far too aware of the teasing gleam in the dark eyes. 'On the surface, yes. But I can't help wondering what lies behind it,' she finished honestly. Jorge had discreetly left them alone in the small sitting-room, and Jane was now looking around her with surprise. White walls, their unevenness hardly hidden by some attractive watercolours, two small but comfy-looking sofas in front of an enormous fireplace that dominated one end of the room. A fire, in deference to the start of autumn, took any chill there might be off the evening air, and all in all it looked an extremely cosy set-up for anyone else but Miguel.

'You know, this just isn't you! Oh, it looks very pretty and homey, but I can't understand why on earth you want to be here,' Jane declared.

'Well, I have an important job to do in this next month, and I needed a base to do it from, so I thought this would be far more fun than a hotel. Come and sit down in front of the fire.'

She did as he asked, but demanded suspiciously, 'What is this job that's going to keep you in Devon for precisely one month?'

'I don't think it would be very wise of me to tell you yet,' he teased, sinking into the sofa opposite her.

Jane couldn't help her colour rising in hurt sympathy. 'I've never before been accused of being indiscreet!' she protested.

'Oh, it's not your discretion I'm worried about,' he answered lazily.

'I'm very good at keeping secrets!' She sat up straight and her eyes challenged him to deny it.

'What a child you still are sometimes!' The flames from the fire reflected on his strong features, giving them a leaping devilish sort of fascination that was shadowed in his eyes. 'But there are some things it is not always possible to hide—one's emotions, for example.' It was difficult for her to read his expression.

'You mean, if you told me your plans, I might unwittingly give them away?' she demanded bluntly.

'Something like that!' he agreed with a smile that grew as he watched her expression. 'Don't worry, sooner or later you'll find out all about it!'

'I shouldn't think I'll be that interested!' she answered haughtily. 'Anyway, what is it you want to talk to me about?'

'I'd like to know your clear, unbiased view of the people you work with,' he asked calmly. 'Whether you think they're any good, and also whether you share my opinion that they're likely to make a success of the whole idea.'

Jane took a deep breath. 'I might have guessed you'd find out that I knew you were my ultimate boss! Did Richard also tell you that I tried to resign when I discovered the truth?'

But it seemed as if she'd miscalculated, because his brows drew together in a formidable frown. 'You knew? How did you find out? Did Richard Alston tell you, or was it one of the others?'

'None of them told me—I found out all by myself!' she answered sarcastically. 'I always thought there was something pretty funny about being picked so quickly for the job, particularly when the competition was so fierce! Why did you set me up?'

For the first time in their relationship Miguel looked a little shifty, and didn't seem to want to meet her eyes. 'It seemed a good idea at the time, particularly as I'd heard that students were finding it hard to get jobs... Richard Alston needed help to get started, so I agreed to help him if he was prepared to take you on and train you at the same time.'

'Why? Why me?' she queried.

He shrugged a little helplessly. 'I knew from Juanita that you were worried about not being able to find a job, and I knew that if we tried to help you your pride would make you throw our offers back in our faces! This seemed a good way round the problem—everyone getting helped at the same time...'

'And you were going to have a lot of fun just now watching my face when I found out you were my boss?' she finished wryly, watching him wriggle uncomfortably in front of her, and was pleased that chance had at last evened things up slightly between them. 'Bad luck, Miguel!' she mocked. 'I'm sorry to have spoiled your fun!'

'I only did it because you're so independent! You have never let Juanita, or any of our family, do anything for you, have you?' He shook his head. 'Strange child! Don't you know that we're all very fond of you? Even my mother and father?'

'Miguel, I really can't see what that has to do with it. Most people learn early in life to stand on their own two feet. Why should I be any different?'

He stood up in a hurry, turning away from her. 'You know why, Jane.'

She looked back at him in astonishment. 'But I don't!' she protested. 'How could I?'

He muttered something under his breath, then turned and pulled her, very ungently, into his arms. 'This is why, you little idiot!' His mouth found hers and she was promptly swept away on a tide of such emotion that there could be no more pretending on her part.

Later, aeons, uncounted time later, he put her gently from him. 'Now look. Jorge may be broad-minded, but I know he will be coming in soon to announce dinner. Also Carmen will not be best pleased if we refuse her best efforts...' He gave her a little shake, his mouth even now still slightly twisted with amusement as he saw how the pupils had spread large and black over her grey eyes.

Jane was acutely embarrassed by the strength of her own reaction to him, particularly when it was he once again who had called a halt to the pro-ceedings. Her limbs were still being shaken by small tremors and she strove valiantly for control. It wasn't fair! Here she was, knocked sideways by his kiss, hardly aware of anything around her, so en-tranced, so transported to another plane had she been, while he, the author of such ecstasy, was able to call a halt, to even still look faintly amused.

She stiffened herself into pretended rejection, loathing the way his looks could reduce her to abject jelly. She cleared her throat, hating the necessity of doing so, but knowing she must still find the strength to fight this physical domination he now had over her.

'I wouldn't dream of giving up Carmen's dinner—I'm feeling extremely hungry because I didn't get much chance of a decent lunch today. Only an apple, to be exact!' she told him. Her eyes had regained some of their challenge, and she noticed a dawning of respect in his face as he con-tinued to look at her steadily. She sat down on the sofa and collected her glass of champagne from the low table at one side. She felt in need of a hefty swig, but managed to disguise it by taking two sips instead.

'Let's hope that dinner will live up to your expectations!' Miguel seemed content to take his tone from hers, so dinner came and went, with both of them touching only on the lightest of subjects until poor Jane was left to wonder if that one kiss between them had been nothing but an extremely erotic dream on her part.

'So, now your job!' Miguel switched the conversation adroitly, as he handed her a cup of coffee. 'Would you like a brandy as well?'

'Heavens, no! I've eaten and drunk enough to last me for at least a week!' she protested.

'Nonsense! That's one of the things I really like about you—you eat normally and sensibly. I can't stand these women who order an expensive dinner, then just pick at it! So do I gather you want to hand in your notice?'

Jane looked at him under her lashes, trying to gauge his reaction if she agreed. 'My immediate reaction was to leave when I found out you owned the company, yes...'

'If I offered you the chance of something a little more exciting, would you consider it?'

It was impossible to hide her interest from this man who watched her every move so carefully, but she could at least control her tongue. 'It would depend what the job entailed; also I'd like to be quite sure that you'd continue to back Richard Alston.'

'Why? What's your interest in him?'

Jane looked at him in surprise. There had been a note in his voice that, if she didn't know better, had almost sounded like jealousy.

'He's a very nice man!' she explained.

'"Very nice men" don't usually succeed in the business world!' he sneered. 'You need guts and a sublime belief in yourself to get to the top!'

'You should know all about that!' she riposted hotly. 'Anyway, why get so uptight? If you hadn't believed in his ultimate success you wouldn't have backed him, would you?'

He looked through her without speaking, as if his thoughts were suddenly far away. 'Are they important to you, these colleagues you work with?'

She was puzzled by his question. 'Not particularly—not personally, no, but that doesn't mean that I'd want to see the company fail just because you decided to pull out.' Her curiosity was almost reaching fever-point. 'What is this job you're thinking of offering me?'

'I need a wife, and I'm afraid I need one in a hurry!' The black eyes were acute and full of his lively intelligence as he studied her reaction to the bombshell he'd just dropped.

Jane thought she now knew what it must feel like to be struck by a bolt of lightning: an instant of incandescent awareness, of knowing that this was paradise spread in front of you; that this was what you wanted more than anything in the world; then the shock, a hundred times more painful than anything yet experienced, that left her feeling numb and empty inside—and yes, emotionally dead.

Like an animal that had been hurt, she lowered her eyes, desperate to hide her pain from the hunter who now loomed so close on her trail.

'Let me explain!' He came to sit next to her, the power and warmth of him almost overpowering her in its intensity. 'This isn't a new idea as far as I'm concerned—it was always something I had in mind since you were seventeen ... I knew I'd meet no one else like you, so you were always to be the one I'd marry. I knew you weren't really as indifferent to me as you pretended this summer, but it was a game I was content to play until you found out how you felt.'

Jane felt as if great bands were tied around her heart, squeezing it tighter and tighter, so that she began to feel light-headed and a little dizzy. Miguel's hand caressed her warm skin, as if he was aware of her inner turmoil and was trying to calm and gentle her.

'But fate has taken a hand and forced me—us—into this present situation. I need you, Jane, very badly. If you'll agree to be my wife then I suggest a civil ceremony. If it doesn't work out, that way you'll be free to try again. I'll see to it, of course, that you won't lose out financially!'

Jane shut her eyes, wondering how anyone could be so indifferent, so unaware of her pain. With an almost colossal effort of will, she made herself ask one vital question. 'Why do you need a wife now?'

The words came out emotionless, cool, surprising her almost as much as they surprised him.

He gave a great sigh. 'Do you remember Patricia, the redhead——?'

She interrupted. 'The president of somewhere's daughter?'

'Yes, that's right.' He looked faintly surprised that she should have remembered. 'El Presidente is trying to twist my arm even further than I'm prepared to go, but "no" won't be taken for answer any more. If I'm to keep that hell-cat at bay I need a legal certificate to prove to her that she's wasting her time. I've told her I'm engaged, but that's not good enough, apparently.'

Jane was still silent, incapable, for the moment, of giving him the answer he seemed to want so desperately. 'Let me take you home now. Tomorrow I'll speak to your parents, warn them of what I have asked of you... Jane, don't let that independence of yours blind you to what I know is true. You want me very much indeed, if that kiss earlier was anything to go by!' His eyes might be gentle as they looked at her, but there was still a teasing gleam in them, as if he was perfectly sure of her answer.

He took hold of both her hands, but the sudden blaze in her big grey eyes stopped him from attempting to kiss her again.

'What happens if I say no?' Her voice sounded light, as if the words were of little importance.

'That could be awkward!' he agreed with a smile.

'You're so sure I'll say yes?' Her voice, soft, so dulcet, caused him to frown.

'But why should you refuse?' he asked, genuinely surprised. 'This is not something I have ever thought of suggesting to anyone else—you know that!'

'You think it's an offer I couldn't say no to?' Jane persisted.

The quick intelligence was working overtime as he looked at her dispassionately, trying, she guessed, to work out his next move.

'Do you care enough for your workmates to safeguard their jobs?' he enquired, his voice smooth and bland.

Her brows rose at the implied threat. Blackmail, no less! He must indeed be desperate if he was resorting to these lengths to get her consent. She guessed it would be extremely wounding to his pride that she hadn't in fact been bending over backwards to accept his proposal.

'If I agreed to marry you, was this supposed to be our honeymoon cottage?' Sure instinct had driven her to cut across his words, to drive right to the heart of the matter.

A rueful grin spread across his face, making him appear somehow more youthful. 'It isn't any good trying to fool you, is it? It never really has been ... You are the only girl I've ever met who I knew I would never be able to bribe into my bed. You don't give a damn for all that money, do you? If anything you find it a turn-off! Don't you see? That's why you're the only girl I've ever met who I want to marry!'

'And you call me contrary!' was forced out of her.

He laughed. 'Say yes, Jane! I promise you won't regret it!'

'Financially maybe not, but I measure life by different standards from you!' she told him firmly.

'Do you doubt that I will be able to make you happy?' There was a fierce pride in his face as he asked that—almost as if he was daring her to deny his undoubted manhood.

She found the strength to return his look. 'Yes, I do doubt exactly that!'

Just for a moment Miguel frowned, not liking her swift response, then, before she could move, or even protest, once more she was in his arms, and his lips were on hers, seeking—no, demanding a response. Her mind might try to scream 'betrayal!' but her body was deaf to its demands, as once more he expertly drew from her a shaming capitulation to his needs that left her in no doubt that she was powerless to refuse whatever he wanted of her.

'Well?' The black eyes, so close to her own, watched the little pulse in her neck race in response to his nearness, and a smile half full of tenderness and triumph lit his face when he saw the surrender on hers. 'Whatever you say, I won't let you regret our marriage!' he told her fiercely, in Spanish. 'Now I'll take you home, and we can break the news to your parents that we are to be married as soon as possible, and hope that they will not be too shocked and surprised at our news.'

'And have you already arranged where we're to be married?' she enquired, and felt a rush of pleasure at the slightly shamefaced look that had crossed his face.

'Yes. Jane, don't look at me like that! I had to do it this way...' There'd been no words of love from him, nothing but a passionate desire on his part for her body, a passion that had somehow grown because of her refusal of him five years ago. This complex man, whose quick brain would always be able to out-think hers, needed a wife. If she turned him down, he'd be upset, but his driving need would force him into his second choice. Knowing him as she did, she didn't doubt that he'd got contingency plans. At least if she was his wife he would be married to someone who loved him and would put his interests first.

'Miguel, if I'm to be forced into marrying you then it's to be done properly, in a church! I'm not interested in half-measures.' She could see he disliked the idea of the word force, but she tilted her chin at him defiantly.

His eyes narrowed. 'Do you mean that? You won't be able to change your mind...'

'Of course I do! I'm a good Catholic girl, remember? Anyway, my parents won't be happy with anything else, and I'm not prepared to marry you at all unless it's done properly!'

She watched him weigh her words, as he balanced her decision against the teaching of their church, which was that the union would be indissoluble if they married in the eyes of God. She knew he was aware that if she had agreed to a civil marriage only, then in the eyes of their church she would be no more than his mistress.

'You want a big wedding?' he demanded, and already she thought she could see that powerful mind working on the logistics.

'No...' she shook her head '...just family in the chapel near here where everyone knows me.'

He took one of her hands and kissed it. 'So be it! You shall be married where you want to. Leave everything else to me.'

Jane looked at him and thought it had to be some deal he'd done with El Presidente, because it was going to cost him his freedom, and that was not something he'd bargained for when he'd first proposed marriage to her. He also promised not to make her regret her hasty marriage to him, but she thought that might be a promise he would find hard to keep in the circumstances.

What could she do against such a man? Nothing, because she'd learnt a long time ago that she wasn't strong enough to stand up to the Tarragos when they wanted something. Then it came to her with all the force of a violent shock. It wouldn't be long before she was a Tarrago herself!

CHAPTER SEVEN

'DO STAND still, child! I'll never be able to get this done on time if you keep on fidgeting so.' Mrs Warren from down the road, who had altered and made dresses for Jane since she was a child, was on her hands and knees trying to pin up the hem of her wedding dress evenly, while Jane's mother fussed around ineffectively, trying not to get in the way.

'Oh, dear, I do hope it's going to be all right! It seems a shame you couldn't have waited to have a dress specially made for you, darling!'

Mrs Warren shook her head indulgently as Mrs Mayfield nearly tripped and fell over her when she stood back trying to get yet another look at her daughter. Jane couldn't help it—she broke out into uninhibited laughter at her mother's affronted face. 'For goodness' sake relax, Mummy! Anyone would think you were going to be the bride, not me!'

'Relax! How can I, when the wedding's on Saturday?'

'But you don't have to do a thing! Miguel's taking care of the reception and everything exactly so you can enjoy yourself and not fuss!'

'And why you both have to get married in such a hurry I'm sure I don't know!' sighed Mrs

Mayfield. 'Why couldn't you get engaged like everyone else?' she demanded.

Jane sighed. 'You know why—we told you! This is just about the only time Miguel has left the whole of this year, and I didn't want to be a fiancée for months and months and have to plan an enormous wedding for all his friends to come to! This is a much nicer way to do things, with just the family...' Her coaxing voice made her mother sigh.

'Well, darling, a week is a very short time, you know, and I can't help thinking it would be better if both of you waited a little longer——'

'But why?' Jane interrupted. 'It's not as though we've only just met. We've known each other for years!'

'Yes, but... Oh, well, I suppose you know your own business best!'

Jane leant over and gave her mother a kiss on the cheek, and tried to contain her own fizzing excitement as she thought of Miguel. 'Stop fussing! You like him, don't you?'

'Oh, yes! He's so very charming...'

Mrs Warren, her mouth still full of pins, joined in. 'She was always in a hurry, even as a child. I can't say this caper of hers surprises me in the least!' Jane giggled, but in truth she too was filled with such a heady mixture of half-frightened excitement that she was almost glad that she had so little leisure to sit and wonder if she was doing the right thing.

Miguel hardly left her side for a second, as if he was intent on being around if she should show any signs of having doubts. Her parents had been charmed but also totally overwhelmed, neither of them able to cope with Miguel's strong personality. That both of them had doubts Jane knew and accepted, realising they weren't at all happy with Miguel's great wealth and how it would affect her. She had done her best to reassure them, but she knew they were not totally happy at the speed with which everything had happened, and in her heart of hearts she agreed with them.

It wasn't much fun either to accept the reasons why he was marrying her so quickly. That if he wasn't being pursued by a rapacious redhead he would still be continuing his slightly amoral and distinctly hedonistic lifestyle without showing the slightest wish to tie himself up in matrimony.

Funnily enough, she believed him when he told her he'd marked her out as his future wife. That was exactly the sort of thing Miguel would do. Leave her to grow up, keep a distant eye on her, and if nothing better came along—well, at some future date when it suited him he would start his courtship, knowing all the time that she was his for the taking.

Put that way it was rather upsetting, which was why, as her wedding-day approached, Jane began to treat him more as a rather frightening stranger, trying desperately to keep him at a distance, as if by doing so she would somehow regain her self-respect.

The day after their engagement was officially endorsed by her family, Miguel came round in the morning to take her out to lunch. Once they were alone in his car, he put his hand in his pocket and threw a small jeweller's box into her lap.

'I hope you'll like my choice, but if you don't it's easily changed.'

Hardly daring to even look at him, Jane opened the box to see a pear-shaped diamond, simply set in platinum, its blue-white radiance sending out great lances of light as the sun caught it. It wasn't enormously large and vulgar, something she'd been afraid of, but exquisitely right for her small hands.

'Oh, Miguel!' She gave him a glance of awe. 'It's beautiful . . .'

He didn't smile, his expression looked rather forbidding as he said, 'Put it on your finger, Jane. I want to see if it looks good on your hand.'

Dutifully she obeyed him, admiring it herself as the sun caught its dazzling purity.

'I hope that'll go some way towards easing your conscience about marrying me!' The faintest of sneers had her head turning smartly towards him, a tide of colour rushing into her cheeks.

'If that's what you think keep it!' Furiously she tore the ring off her finger, and without looking at it again fumbled it back into its box. 'There!' She tossed it contemptuously back into his lap.

Miguel braked the car off the road on to a broad grass verge. 'You're my future wife, and I expect you to try and conform to my wishes! You agreed to be my wife, remember?' he reminded her stiffly.

'I too had hoped my future husband would behave with dignity and good manners!' Jane flashed back at him. 'But perhaps I shouldn't be too surprised. Anyone who has to compel someone to be his wife by uttering threats...' There was a moment of prickly silence, with him looking at her with an expression of cold indifference.

'You don't wish to continue with our agreement?'

'You know damn well I don't! But I have to, don't I? Otherwise innocent people might lose their jobs...'

'You'd do well to remember exactly that!' Miguel told her, and his voice now had a firm ring of steel in it. 'Put this ring back on. It's part of the deal.'

'Are you sure there's nothing more? No more strings you wish to pull to make me dance to your tune?' There was a mocking twist to her mouth as she looked up at him.

'Not at the moment, no...' He looked down at her, his eyes cold and considering. 'But don't worry, I'll let you know soon enough if I find anything!'

'I bet you will!' she muttered, but it was hard to hide her pain at his callous indifference to her feelings.

The day his family was due to arrive from Spain he took her out on to Dartmoor, as if by escaping the confines of family in that vast great loneliness they could become closer to each other. Hugely energetic, he had her walking along little-used sheep paths, stumbling clumsily in his wake, the skylarks singing against a vault of the clearest blue, the golden bracken a background for further great tracts of heather that spread around them.

Miguel had set his heart on achieving a small tor which looked as if it should command distant views

once attained. Jane, born and brought up so near
the Moor, was surprised he should have set up such
a cracking pace until she realised that this was the
whole pattern of his life: set a goal, then achieve
it as fast as possible, before setting out on new aims,
new journeys. Still, she hadn't realised that he was
quite so fit...

On each side bees buzzed, taking the last of the
honey from the purple bell-shaped flowers of the
heather. 'Miguel,' she protested. 'Must you go at
quite such a speed?'

He slowed down, allowing her to catch up with
him, then took one of her hands. 'Are you tired?
I'll give you a hand...'

'No! Just stop a moment, will you, and look
around?' She pulled her hand free of his, and gestured towards the heather and the tireless bees who
worked so assiduously looking for its sweetness,
then up to the heavens where the skylarks sang their
own sweet song. 'Isn't it beautiful?' she breathed.
'When I go out for a walk I like to be able to appreciate the flowers, to stop and listen to the
birds...'

'Yes, but we're not there yet! Come on. We'll see
much more higher up!'

Fiercely she turned to face him.

'Why can't you see the beauty right here and
now? Why do we have to climb to that tor?'

'Come on, Jane! The higher you get, always the
more beautiful the view!'

'No, not necessarily more beautiful, just more of
it! But you miss so much on the way by walking

so fast. If you took it a little more slowly I could appreciate all these small country things I love so much...'

'Love...' Miguel said slowly. 'What do you know of love, little innocent?' He took her head in his hands and his lips teased hers until he felt her respond, then he pulled her close to him, so close that she could feel the tumultuous beating of his heart, his determined strength and the half-intolerable ecstasy of his passionate kiss. Such an expert kiss too, one that seemed to demand that she surrender her very soul to his arrogant demands. Hurt pride, and a very real fear that if she allowed him to walk freely all over her it would mean that never in the future would they be able to establish an equal relationship, had her pulling away, ending the kiss far sooner than he had intended.

'But why, *querida*?' he asked.

Jane had to harden her heart at his expression. He seemed so confident, so sure of her continued response to his lovemaking. He moved to pull her back close to him, so sure of her melting response that for once she saw him looking totally disconcerted as she moved out of his reach.

'No, Miguel!' Just for a moment everything hung in the balance between them, and Jane guessed he was not too used to having the initiative taken away from him, particularly when he had been so certain that he was in command of her every mood.

'So we wait...' A slow smile lit his eyes, and she was surprised to see yet again that dawning of respect at her refusal to give in to his wishes. She followed him on up the path, this time happily, knowing that for once she had done the right thing. He could change so quickly, this man of hers, one moment the teasing lover, the next a cold stranger as she defied him. Her deeper reasons for continuing this charade between them she kept firmly hidden. If he ever found out he had gained her heart then she would be lost forever.

Two days later she was the Señora Miguel de Tarrago, married by Father Beale in the tiny chapel where she was used to hearing Mass—almost unrecognisably transformed by the wonderful flower arrangements—in front of only their immediate families.

Her mother and Juanita cried, although Jane could scarcely believe it was for the same reasons, and she became aware that her husband was looking down at her with an expression of pride and possession on his face. The passion was there, but veiled, half hidden in the dark eyes, yet she could feel its controlled power waiting to be unleashed at the appropriate moment. But there were no signs that he loved her.

Her cheeks were covered in a hectic flush that owed nothing to champagne. Her stimulant stood next to her, claiming his own with arrogant ease in front of his family. When Carlos walked forward to greet her with the customary kiss on each cheek, she noticed that Miguel disliked him greeting his bride.

'Jane!' He smiled brilliantly at her, ignoring Miguel. 'Soon you will be my sister, yes?'

She smiled back at him. 'I suppose I will!' she agreed.

A more serious expression crossed his face. 'You have forgiven me, I hope? I behaved so badly the last time we met, and I have wanted for a long time to make my apologies to you in person. Juanita and I——' he clasped his fiancée's hand tightly '—were so happy when we heard the news. You deserve your happiness. Miguel, you are a very lucky man.'

'Believe me, Carlos, I know it!' Her husband's dark, enigmatic eyes met hers for a single moment, but what they promised had her feeling dizzy.

'What an unusual dress, Jane!' Juanita greeted her in her usual critical manner, her eyes taking in every detail of the simple dress, so obviously not a couture creation.

'But exactly what I wanted!' her new sister-in-law told her with a smile.

'I like the cross. Did Miguel give it to you?' Juanita enquired, still busy with her inventory.

'No.' Jane shook her head and smiled. 'No, that belonged to my grandmother.'

'Oh?' Jane had to smile at Juanita's surprised expression. 'What has Miguel given you? Apart from your engagement ring, that is...' she continued, managing effectively to wipe the smile off her face. Jane had indeed been given an embarrassingly grand set of jewellery by her new parents-in-law, but from Miguel himself she had had nothing except the gold band that now circled her finger so strangely.

'Don't worry, *pequeña*! I haven't forgotten you.' His voice, smooth, amused, took over. 'My presents to Jane are certainly going to be worth waiting for, Nita! But this has been such a sudden decision on our part that I was not properly prepared!'

Typically Juanita fastened on to the one potentially awkward question. 'Yes!' she answered eagerly. 'Why have you married Jane in such a hurry? Why couldn't you have waited? Poor Jane, you have stopped her from having a big wedding like mine!'

Miguel picked up his wife's small hand and pressed a warm kiss into the palm, a gesture of such intimacy that it heightened her colour. 'You ask why I couldn't wait!' His eyes were full of amusement and something deeper as he looked into Jane's grey ones, forcing her to hold them until her blush deepened uncomfortably and she broke the contact. He laughed, then looked back at his sister, who was frowning at him. 'That's why, Nita! I hope you don't expect me to spell it out any further?'

'Don't bully, Miguel! Jane doesn't like it.' Jane was surprised to see that Juanita was looking really upset. Her brother raised his eyebrows, as if she'd made some remark in questionable taste.

'Juanita, I've always managed my own affairs very nicely without your help.' As a put-down, Jane had heard much worse, so she was surprised when she saw the dull flush that covered Juanita's olive skin, and saw how her black eyes glittered.

'Don't underrate her, Miguel! She's not a girl who likes to be intimidated, nor will she ever look up to you as some kind of god like those others you used to run around with!'

Jane noticed with dismay that Miguel looked absolutely furious. 'Hey, this is supposed to be my wedding-day!' She gave his sleeve a sharp tug, before turning to give Juanita a placatory smile. 'Darling, don't fight my battles for me! You should know I'm quite capable of fighting my own when I put my mind to it!'

'What's all this talk about fighting?' Jane's new father-in-law came to stand next to her. 'That sounds ominous.'

'Don't worry, Papá!' Juanita took his arm. 'It was a quarrel between brother and sister, not husband and wife.' She stopped for dramatic effect. 'Yet...' She gave her brother a quick flashing glance before walking away.

Miguel took in an explosive breath. 'That girl! Carlos has taken on quite a handful—she's become impossibly spoilt!'

Jane looked at him, her head a little on one side. 'No, only a little too accustomed to having her own way, like her brother!' Once again it seemed to Jane that her words had balanced them both on the edge of something unspoken between them, and this time she flinched inwardly at the coldness in those dark eyes that were staring down at her with such level concentration.

There was no sign this time that he found her words even remotely amusing, or indeed anything

but a threat to his future plans. Quite uncon-
sciously Jane found herself sticking out her chin a
little in unspoken defiance. Perhaps it was no bad
thing that they were interrupted at this point by
Father Beale, whose happy good nature was quite
incapable of understanding that the new husband
and wife had just had an unresolved tussle of wills.
His benign presence was enough to ensure that for
the moment, at least, nothing would be put into
words, and maybe that was all for the best, Jane
thought a little unhappily, as she and Miguel gave
every pretence of being the happy couple that
everyone expected them to be.

The hotel at which Miguel had chosen to have
the reception after his wedding, and to put up his
family, had once been an old manor house, and its
rooms were well suited to their present use. It had
all been quite beautifully organised, and the lunch
provided exceptional, as the families relaxed
together in the private suite that overlooked a fast-
flowing river; but to Jane and, she thought, her
mother, it lacked reality. It was too beautiful, too
smoothly arranged, so that there was a dreamlike
air around it.

Jane sat, wondering just exactly what she had
got herself into, refusing to meet her mother's eyes,
except in the most fleeting manner, listening to
Juanita's plans for her own wedding to take place
later that year in Madrid, while Miguel, next to her,
was outwardly the same as ever, although deep
inside she knew he was brooding over what had
just happened between them. Did he really think

she would subjugate herself so utterly and entirely
to his will? Juanita certainly seemed to think that
that was what he would expect of her, but she found
it hard to believe. She was no little 'yes-girl', and
if anyone knew that then Miguel did. Was he hoping
to coerce her with physical ties? It was no use to
go on thinking about it. Today she was married,
for better, for worse, and there was absolutely
nothing she could do about it.

'Regretting your marriage already?' She wasn't
altogether prepared for his perspicacity as his dark
eyes zeroed in on her face.

'Should I be?' she demanded, knowing that she
was on uncertain ground now that he seemed to
want to put their unspoken battle into words. But
once again she was to be saved by circumstance.
Her father stood up to make a toast, and the
moment was lost. Her half-frightened excitement
had intensified, and she wondered if any other bride
had felt her curious mixture of emotions, as the
speeches rang in her head.

Changed, and ready to leave, she sought the
comfort of her husband's presence, trying hard to
forget Juanita's parting words and their bitterness
of spirit against her once so beloved brother.

Juanita had attacked her when they were alone
together in the bedroom upstairs. 'Why did you do
it, Jane?' she had demanded bitterly. 'I thought you
at least would never settle for second best! He
doesn't love you, and I'm not even sure now if you
love him... There's something horribly wrong between the two of you, and I don't know what it is.'

There had been no time for her to say any more, but it had been quite enough to destroy Jane's peace of mind. Deliberately she forced the words into the back of her mind.

She even ensured that her wedding bouquet should fall into Juanita's hands as she tossed it carefully at her new sister-in-law, who was standing outside on the steps with the rest of their families to watch them leave. No one had the slightest clue that she was not leaving for some distant and extremely exotic location, but just simply an old Devon long-house not so very far away.

Jane, aware that it didn't really matter where she spent her honeymoon, because her future as Miguel's wife would entail many journeys to foreign lands, was in fact quite happy to stay in the county where she had been born and had grown up. Anyway, by now all she could think of was being possessed by her husband, and she hoped he would forget their little unspoken disagreement and become just as passionately obsessed with their immediate future as she was, and it seemed she needn't worry as he turned to speak to her.

'Four in the afternoon is an awkward time to fill, particularly if one has just had a large lunch, don't you think?' He gave her a lazy smile. 'I think the best thing would be if we both rested until dinner.' His eyes and voice were warmly suggestive of what it would entail if she took him up on his offer.

Grateful for the way he made it appear quite normal that they should consider retiring to bed as soon as they arrived, Jane gave him a smile that had so much promise in it that he trod firmly on the accelerator.

The Porsche responded with leaping power as Miguel concentrated on getting them back to their secluded cottage fast. It was sheer bad luck that the old tractor and trailer lurched out without looking on to the tiny road in front of them, and Miguel didn't have a chance, although his reactions were as quick as a cat's. Jane sat with horrified eyes watching and waiting for the inevitable, which seemed to last for eternity. There was no time to scream, no time for anything, as the gleaming metal of the Porsche ploughed into the rusty rear of the trailer with an appalling bang.

The trailer began to collapse under the impact. A huge chunk of rusty metal came crashing through the windscreen, hitting Miguel hard on the left side of his head. A dark explosion now totally engulfed Jane's own senses as she slid away into semi-consciousness, half convinced her husband had to be dead.

She couldn't breathe properly; as she tried to take a deeper breath the pain in her chest increased sufficiently to wake her up. 'Oh, God,' she muttered, 'help me!' Slowly and with trembling fingers she undid her seatbelt, then, terrified of what she would find, turned her head towards Miguel.

She moaned in terror. The huge chunk of metal lay between them, and behind it Miguel lay, crushed and somehow diminished by his unconsciousness. Every move she tried to make seemed to stab her,

the pain making it impossible for her to breathe
except in the shallowest way possible. Fear and
helpless terror that Miguel was dead forced her to
further efforts, but it was hopeless. She was trapped
in her seat until help arrived. Miguel could be
bleeding to death inches away from her, and there
would be nothing she could do about it. All she
had been able to do was grope until she found his
hand, warm and seemingly lifeless, and this she
clung on to while tears poured soundlessly from
her eyes as she prayed.

Help arrived, but how long it took to get to them
she was never to know, and it was to him that she
directed their best efforts.

'I'm all right, don't bother about me! It's my
husband . . .' she had pleaded with one of the local
fire brigade.

'Don't worry, we're taking care of him, miss—
er—madam. Now, if you could just . . .'

She did all that they asked her, but her interest
lay entirely with Miguel and whether he was still
alive. She almost passed out with relief when the
paramedic told her he thought he was only badly
concussed.

Soon free herself, she was told she had two
probable broken ribs and a severely bruised
sternum. 'Typical seatbelt injuries!' she was told
by the ambulanceman as they sped on their way to
the local big casualty hospital, but she was far more
worried about Miguel and his continued coma, and
tears ran down her face as she refused to be
comforted.

After being treated and X-rayed, she was told she was to stay in one night just to ensure there were no complications. Up in the ward she was free for the first time to use a telephone.

It was no use calling her own parents. Her father had used her wedding as an excuse to take her mother away for the weekend on a break. She would have to call the hotel where they'd had the reception and hope that her father-in-law would still be there. Shock had made her so woozy that the sister had to help her find the number, but she was lucky. Papá was still there, and after his first horrified exclamation he assured her that he would take care of everything, she was not to worry about a thing.

The first intimation she had of just that was when she was woken from a light doze she'd sunk into by a posse of white coats surrounding her bed.

'Señora de Tarrago?' A tall, grey-haired, very eminent-looking man was addressing her.

'Who? Oh, sorry—er—yes?' She tried to pull her scattered wits together, but couldn't help wincing as she tried to move.

'Please, *señora*, don't try to move!' A smile and placating arm were stretched out to her, but she refused to be comforted.

'Is it Miguel?' Her face looked pathetically pinched and pale as she tried to brace herself for his answer.

'No, no, my dear! Your husband has recovered consciousness, so you've no need to worry about him!'

Jane thought his answer a bit too hearty, as if he was overdoing the not to worry bit, but she still felt dizzy and not at all with it, so was prepared to let it go for the moment. She lay back on her pillows with a sigh of relief.

'I've been asked by your father-in-law to check you over before we move you to a private clinic tomorrow...'

'Private clinic?' she echoed. 'I don't need to go to a clinic!'

'Your father-in-law is a bit concerned that you have nowhere to go except a hotel room.'

Jane shut her eyes. 'No, I'll be all right, truly. We have a cottage near the edge of the Moor... Tell Papá that Carmen and Jorge are there. Oh, God! Someone must ring them. They'll be wondering what on earth has happened!' she wailed.

'Gently, my dear—we'll do that,' the man told her. 'Do you have the number?'

'Yes, I suppose so. It's in my bag. I can't remember it off-hand—my brain seems to have gone all woozy...' Suddenly everything became too much of a strain, and Jane turned her head on to the pillow and shut her eyes. That still didn't stop the tears from oozing out in a slow trickle.

'Try to relax, *señora* ... Now I'm going to give you something that will ensure you have a good night's sleep!' She hardly felt the prick of the injection, and soon she had drifted away into another world where nothing hurt any more.

She woke up the next morning to discover that she had been moved into a small amenity ward

SOMETHING WORTH FIGHTING FOR

overnight, and the whole room was absolutely full
of flowers. She also discovered that broken ribs
were extremely painful, even the smallest of movements assuming major proportions in her mind as
she tried to ignore the pain.

'Good morning, Señora de Tarrago!' A pretty
blonde-haired woman put her head round the door.
'I'm your special nurse. How are you feeling
today?'

'Not too bad, if I don't move!' Jane grimaced.

'We'll soon take care of that, then you can think
about breakfast.'

'Can you tell me how my husband is?' Jane asked
anxiously.

'He's had a reasonable night, and he's out of
danger,' the nurse told her.

'Oh, thank goodness!' Jane's eyes filled with
tears.

'Yes, you can relax, the worst is over. Now, let's
get you up, shall we?' The blonde nurse became
smoothly professional, but after an hour or so of
her ministrations Jane began to rebel.

To start with, she made her do things that hurt—
really hurt, and she never stopped asking ques-
tions, half of which she answered herself, but even
so her voice was irritating. It was very kind of Papá
de Tarrago to order her a private nurse, but quite
frankly she didn't want one. She wanted first of all
to see Miguel, then to be allowed to go back to the
cottage with Carmen and Jorge to look after her.

In the end she lost her patience. 'Please, Nurse—
I want to see my husband, now! Either you take

me, or I'll find my own way!' she snapped. At least the pain-killers she'd been given had reduced the pain to a background nuisance just as long as she was careful. She stood up in her own nightdress and dressing-gown, which had been sent to the hospital, and gave the nurse a fierce look.

'I—well, I... Look, I'll have to ring the doctor who was in charge of his case. You can speak to him yourself. OK?'

Jane agreed, but suspiciously. Something was wrong somewhere, but she couldn't quite work out why or what. She waited until she heard her nurse talking, telling someone unseen that she insisted on being taken to see her husband, then there was a small silence, with the nurse just agreeing with the unseen doctor. She put the phone down and turned to Jane.

'The consultant is coming to see you himself in about half an hour. I hope that's all right?'

Jane was puzzled as well as suspicious. 'You did say my husband was in no danger?' she queried.

'Absolutely! You don't want to worry about that!' Jane thought the nurse sounded almost too cheerful, as if she was hiding something from her, but if Miguel wasn't dangerously ill then it couldn't be anything serious, could it?

'You're sure?' she queried again. 'I mean, you're not trying to keep me happy or anything like that?'

The nurse looked shocked. 'I don't tell lies, Señora de Tarrago. You can be quite sure that your husband is in no danger. He has suffered superficial bruising, and has a broken rib like yourself, but his concussion isn't worrying his doctor, I do assure you!'

The nurse left her alone after that, and Jane sat upright in her chair, staring unseeingly at the wonderful flowers, her mind trying to work out just exactly why Miguel wasn't demanding to see her. She knew her husband well enough to know that if he wished to see her she would have been with him before now, whatever his injuries. So why?

Her reverie was disturbed by the return of the urbane consultant she'd met last night, but this time he was accompanied by Papá de Tarrago.

'Papá!' she called breathlessly, before a couple of twinges reminded her of the unwisdom of expanding her lungs.

'Darling!' He came over to kiss her cheek. 'What a drama! Thank God you're both more or less OK!' There was an expression on his face that she didn't quite understand as he looked down at her.

'Jane . . .' he held one of her hands lightly in his own '. . . Miguel has no memory of the last three weeks of his life. We don't know if he will ever remember, or if the memory will return quite quickly. Either way——' he squeezed her hands comfortingly '—he does not know you are now his wife!'

'But can't you tell him?' Jane implored.

'We have.' It was the consultant's turn to speak. 'I'm afraid he denies that there ever could be a possibility of his marrying you.'

Jane went white, and lay back in her chair. So this was the ultimate, the final irony, and Juanita had been quite right after all when she'd insisted Miguel didn't, couldn't be in love with her—that she, Jane, had been a fool to allow herself to be used as a part of his selfish demands. If you love someone, how can you forget it? she asked herself. Her heart gave her the answer, and she bit back a sob. She closed her eyes and began to think, to plan; anything rather than add to the pain she was feeling.

'Papá!' Her grey eyes fixed on his face. 'You'd better start arranging an annulment . . .'

'But my dear!' He looked horrified. 'Once Miguel is better, is more in his right mind, this problem will go away!'

'No!' She shut her eyes again, but not before the two men saw her agony. 'No . . . He married me as an expediency, a solution to the problem of Patricia. He didn't want a church wedding, just a civil ceremony, but I insisted on doing everything properly . . .' She gave a great sigh. 'It was a mistake—I see that now. He should get his annulment without too much trouble, shouldn't he?' she appealed to his father.

'Darling, don't make these sort of decisions now! You aren't well enough——'

But she interrupted Papá. 'No, I'm right. You think this is just the result of shock from the accident, but it isn't! I sort of knew beforehand that it was wrong . . .' She appealed once more to him. 'You'll help me, won't you?'

'But, my dear, this is madness! If only we could get in touch with your father and mother, but, as you know, they've gone away and aren't expected home until late this evening. They'll tell you I am right. This is no time to take such a decision. Why, in a month's time, you'll look back and laugh at this time!'

'No,' Jane answered sadly, 'no, I don't think so. Why don't you ask Miguel for his views? I think you'll find that he'll agree with me!'

Papá de Tarrago tried to bluster his way out, but he couldn't fool Jane. She gave him a sad smile. 'I see he's already suggested it!'

'He doesn't know what he is saying! He is not in his right mind! Believe me, Jane——' he held up on finger in front of her '—when he recovers, starts to think again properly and coolly, you'll see! He will still want his wife—mark my words!'

'But maybe I don't want him any more,' she finished sadly.

'Now that's not true! You love my son very much, and we have all been so happy at your marriage. You must know how difficult it is for people in our position to find love.' His eyes, quizzical and amused, reminded Jane painfully of Miguel's. 'And one thing we have always known is that you would never marry Miguel for his money... My son is ill. We cannot expect him to think and behave rationally until he is better, and, my dear, I want you to understand this and behave sensibly until he has recovered.'

'How can I?' she sighed. 'Miguel has always known his own mind. If he's made up his mind to deny that our marriage has happened, then that's what he will do! Anyway, no one knows about it.'

'Unfortunately that's true,' Papá agreed. 'The notices have not yet been sent to the papers. Miguel wanted a few days' peace before the paparazzi were on your trail! Which reminds me——' he looked at the consultant '—what about the security here?'

'I don't think you need worry too much. Your name is not at all well-known in this country, so I can't see anyone bothering the papers.'

'Maybe...' Papá mused. 'Jane, my dear daughter—because that is how I will now always think of you—I think it will be better for you to go to your parents to continue the rest of your convalescence. We are flying Miguel back to Madrid tomorrow. Our own doctor is on his way over here now, and he will supervise his transfer. Once we are sure you are quite better, then we will send the plane back over for you, so you may come home!'

Jane smiled weakly through her tears at the triumph on Papá's face. He thought he'd got everything so nicely organised—Miguel brainwashed into remembering what he'd so conveniently forgotten, then, when they were sure he wouldn't reject her outright, she'd be returned to her husband, then hopefully nature would take over. It would be so easy just to fall in with these plans, but Jane knew she couldn't do it. She would only return if her husband loved her—a forlorn hope maybe—otherwise she would wait for her marriage to be annulled.

CHAPTER EIGHT

THREE weeks later Jane got the expected summons to Spain. Her mother and father, although horrified by the accident, were of the same opinion as the Tarragos: namely that the marriage was an accomplished fact, and there could be no point in denying it. Anyway, she for her part knew it would now be virtually impossible to tell her parents that she thought it would be better ended.

Her mother, once she'd got over the shock, had been quite pleased to have her daughter returned to her, even if it was only temporarily.

'Oh, my darling, think how awful it would be if Miguel had been killed!' she had said to Jane on her return to her old home. Of course, that had been all that was needed to set Jane off into a fit of weeping, but curiously, once it was over, she had felt better, more able to cope with her problems.

Only a day after Miguel had returned to Spain the news had been released to the media, also with the news of the accident. Their wedding photos were given to the Press and, if they did not rate very highly at home, in Spain they were front-page news. Jane had been cross about this, thinking it was another tactic of Papá's to force Miguel's hand, but he had denied it, so in the end she had come to the conclusion that it had been done to protect Miguel from Patricia.

As this had been the whole point of their marriage in the first place it was hard to understand why she should feel such outrage at her own logical thoughts. She felt she had trapped herself, and, although these last weeks had given her time to try and come to terms with herself, all it had done was highlight her dilemma. She was in love with her husband, had married him indeed without him once admitting that he loved her in return, half of her so desperate to be his wife that she'd ignored the danger signals of which her other half had been all too aware.

Because she'd heard no direct word from Miguel since the accident, she was more than half inclined to believe Juanita's last embittered attack as they'd left their wedding reception. Even her own family found it strange that among the constant calls from Spain not one was from her husband.

What she was told by Papá and Miguel's consultant was quite different. They told her that her husband was making a slow recovery, but had been plagued by very bad headaches. He found it very difficult to concentrate, and was exceedingly irritable with everybody, which was why, apart from his doctor, he was not disturbed more than necessary. Rest and relaxation, she'd been told, were what was needed, and no excitement.

'Darling!' Papá had rung very excitedly a week after their return. 'Miguel's remembered——'

'Remembered our wedding-day?' Jane had interrupted breathlessly.

'No, not that. But he certainly now recalls his journey to the West Country.'

'Oh! Does he remember why he came over?' asked Jane.

'I'm not sure; we haven't discussed details, but I should think so. Be happy, my dear—this is a start after all!' It had been pointless to be too upset, but if Miguel had remembered his reasons for marrying her at least that was an advance, even if she couldn't get too excited by it.

At first she'd refused to consider going to Spain until she had a specific invitation to do so from her husband, but, on hearing that in the doctor's opinion she could materially benefit Miguel's final recovery, she'd been forced to accept that she had little alternative to acceding to the Tarragos' demands that she finally return home.

She was touched to find that when the executive jet landed at Exeter airport Juanita was in it, having come all the way just to ensure that Jane would not feel too strange and alone on her return to Spain.

After a tearful farewell to Jane's parents, the two girls embraced, boarded the plane and Juanita burst out, 'Oh, Jane! I've felt so bad about what I told you after the wedding. I don't always understand Miguel, it's true, and then this awful accident ...'

'Forget it!' Jane suddenly felt considerably older than her sister-in-law. 'Either way it's of no importance any more, is it?'

'I suppose so... Oh, Jane, they don't think he will ever remember marrying you!'

'How much does he remember?' she couldn't help querying. 'No one has really answered that question.'

'The truth is none of us really knows,' Juanita admitted. 'He's OK about pretty nearly everything, except that last trip of his to England to find you. He remembers flying into Exeter airport, but I think he's pretty hazy about what happened afterwards. You know what he's like! He doesn't talk about anything that worries him... I think his doctor wants you to try to jog his memory about that time to see if it helps him, because of course it's that loss of memory that's worrying him so much.'

'Oh, lord! I suppose he's frightened I somehow trapped him into this marriage?' asked Jane.

'He hasn't said so—at least not in my hearing. He spends lots of time looking at the wedding pictures and the video recording in the chapel.'

'Seeing is believing, I suppose...' Jane gave a large sigh. 'I still think it might be the best answer to have the whole thing annulled as I originally suggested.'

Juanita gave her a horrified look, but after a severe inner struggle contented herself with saying, 'Well, don't be too hard on him! He still isn't able to work properly, you know. He can't concentrate for long, and he still gets these awful headaches.'

'But I thought he was supposed to be fine?' Juanita picked up her worry and fear.

'He is really. I mean, it's nothing to worry about, all quite normal, apparently, but head injuries take time.' Juanita's voice sounded surprisingly comforting with its extreme confidence.

'I thought he was dead in the car, you know...' Jane couldn't stop herself reliving those awful moments before they had been freed, and shuddered in memory.

'Don't!' Juanita pleaded. 'It must have been awful. I try to imagine what I would have felt if it was Carlos, because you really do love Miguel, don't you?'

Jane gave her a whimsical smile. 'Yes, I'm afraid I do... Silly of me, isn't it?'

'No. This time you must make quite sure he realises just how much he loves you! No half-measures. He was always interested, even from that first year you came to stay with us, when you were only twelve or thirteen, so it shouldn't be too difficult to catch him now he's off guard, should it?'

'Easier said than done!' Jane answered sharply, wondering how on earth Juanita could think Miguel would be easier to handle in his present state. She guessed he would be twice as wary of her, already being deeply suspicious of how she'd become his wife.

'He's really had quite a hard time these last weeks!' Juanita mused. 'He doesn't seem so arrogantly confident any more, for a start. Maybe losing his memory has been traumatic in more ways than one. He's always asking me about you—little things, you know... It's weird! I mean, if I didn't know him better, I'd almost say he's scared stiff of meeting you again! By the way, before I forget, I have a letter for you from Miguel's doctor. He wants you to read it, then get in touch with him, OK?'

Not unnaturally Juanita's remarks about Jane's husband being scared to meet her were puzzling, but Jane managed to steer the conversation back to Juanita's own wedding in one month's time. Fortunately, after that, her sister-in-law insisted on trying to sleep as there was a party in Madrid that night that she didn't want to miss, and left Jane alone to read her letter.

Jane read it twice, each time deeply disturbed by the contents. The doctors seemed to think that there were other reasons, apart from the accident, why Miguel chose not to remember the three weeks that led up to his wedding. They also seemed to think that she would know why he should be blocking out this period of his life. They suggested that some deep-seated stress was the problem and that his subconscious had used the concussion to bury what he would find painful to remember.

Her thoughts, sad and jumbled, occupied her mind fully until just before they were due to land at Palma airport. The stewardess's words brought her back to the present.

'Palma?' Jane queried. 'I thought we were going to Madrid?'

It was Juanita who answered, still sleepily stretching after her catnap.

'No, it was Miguel himself who chose to come back to the island to recuperate. Goodness only knows why! It upset all Mamá's plans, and she has to be in Madrid so much for the wedding. I think she's quite pleased that you're coming to take her place!' she finished mischievously as she watched Jane's face. 'I have to get back there myself, so the two of you will be left all alone, except for Carmen and Jorge, just as he originally planned it for you!'

'You mean there's no one at the villa but the two of us?' Jane said, her voice faintly horrified.

'Just exactly that!' Juanita agreed with a smile. 'You don't even need to worry about Miguel's health either. If he gets one of his headaches he just takes a pill and lies down until it goes.' She hugged Jane. 'I expect to see the two of you at my wedding, but not before!'

Feeling more and more like a sacrificial lamb, Jane sat, stiff and uncomfortable, in the back seat of the big grey Mercedes. One of the bodyguards sat in the front next to Jorge, reminding her of the reality of being a Tarrago. From now on she would be a bit like royalty, never really alone.

She wondered how she could have forgotten irritating small things like this while she was with Miguel. She'd certainly given up her freedom when she'd allowed him to put that gold ring on her finger. Then she took herself to task. She should be thinking of about him, not herself, surely?

But she couldn't help thinking about that great gilded cage which was about to close around her.

Maybe it would be bearable if she were to share it with someone who loved her, but that daydream had become more and more unlikely as each day had passed without a word from her husband.

She had no doubt that the stress-induced amnesia was a result of their getting married, and the only way she could think of to relieve him of it was to insist on a final separation. It would be very hard for her, but, as long as he never knew she loved him, maybe it would be bearable.

They met again high up on the terrace, and it was Jane who had to make the effort to find Miguel, not the other way about, which she took to be an ominous sign. At first sight she was horrified to see how much weight he had lost, and his new, slimmer outline made him appear younger. His hair too had been closely cropped, but was still not long or thick enough to hide the scars where he'd been hit in the accident.

His eyes, dark and opaque, defied her searching glances, revealing nothing of his thoughts. So still and wooden was his expression that she felt half repelled. Here was nothing remotely welcoming, and she felt a despairing chill. This was rejection, no less, but she was too proud to wait for him to put it into words. Defiantly she allowed him to see nothing of her pain. Why should he be allowed to know that he'd won her heart after all?

'I see you agree with me that an annulment is the only answer to this mess,' she told him, her voice sounding hard and brittle.

Something flashed deep in the dark depths of his eyes, but before she could work out what it meant he had turned casually away to look out to sea.

'If that's what you want,' he answered flatly.

'It isn't a question of what I want, is it?' she hissed at him, hurt and resentment piercing her fragile shell of indifference. 'It never has been what I want as far as you're concerned. You married me, whether you remember it or not, to save yourself from the attentions of some president's daughter. It wasn't because you loved me, or even particularly wanted me. I was just suitable. A girl you'd known since she was a child, and someone you knew who wasn't a gold-digger! I don't quite know what you had planned for us as a couple, but one thing I am sure of—my feelings wouldn't have been allowed to count with you at all. I amused you by being different from the rest of the girls you knew, but once I was your wife you'd stop being amused pretty quickly if I didn't do exactly what you wanted when you wanted!'

'Why did you marry me, then?' His voice, now cool and controlled, stopped her in her tracks. Six little words that required an answer, and how was she to get round that without telling the truth?

'You know perfectly well why!' she attacked in response.

'All the same, I'd rather hear it from you,' Miguel insisted politely.

'You made love to me, knowing that I... Oh, why should I tell you any more?' she cried.

He turned swiftly to face her. 'Since you're so squeamish, I'll finish it for you! You resent me because I can make you physically want me. I suppose you think I trapped you into this marriage, rather than the reverse? That's the truth, isn't it?'

She searched his face, but there were no clues to be found on its guarded visage. 'Yes, you trapped me into marriage, but not for that reason. And yes, I do—I did feel resentful at the way you could make me feel, but that isn't the whole reason either. These are all different parts of what's wrong between us, but...' she gave him a fierce look '...I did not trap you!'

'Don't lie, Jane! I can see myself offering to marry you in a civil ceremony, because that's what I always envisaged myself doing, but I think it's highly unlikely I would have agreed to marry you in church unless you had a very compelling reason to force me to do so. Are you pregnant? Or did you conveniently lose the baby in the accident?'

'That's a filthy thing to say or even think!' Jane was almost in tears.

'Why do you keep splitting hairs, pretending so?' Miguel demanded bitterly. 'All women are the same! They don't like to face reality, so it has to be dressed up, prettied up... Talk about love, when they mean desire. Talk about security, when they mean greed. Being emotionally deprived if they don't have a man dancing attendance on them twenty-four hours a day! Believe me, I've been through all that; heard all the excuses...

'I still don't know why I married you, and I hope, if you stay here, that perhaps your presence might help me to find out just what it was, because I could have sworn that marriage was the last thing on my mind!'

Jane looked at him with shocked disbelief. Never before had she heard him sound so bitter, so disillusioned. If this was what he was hiding inside, then no wonder marriage had been the last thing on his mind!

What was she to do? Stay here alone with this stranger? Did she in fact have any choice in the matter? She was Miguel's wife in the eyes of the church and the law in a strongly Catholic country. If he wanted her to stay here, she didn't think he would allow her to go. She veiled her eyes, unwilling for him to see how much he had hurt her.

'Is that all you want me to do?' she demanded. 'Just stay here in the same house with you?'

'Is that all you're prepared to offer? I had thought, now that we are man and wife——'

She interrupted him fiercely, hating the sarcastic tone in his voice, knowing that somehow he blamed her for his present predicament, 'No! Never while you feel like this... File for an annulment. Little though you seem to believe it, I can assure you our marriage has never been consummated, in or out of wedlock!'

'You're still a virgin?' She surprised the first raw emotion on his face since her arrival, until once more he had his features under guard.

'Yes!' she mocked. 'Hard to believe, isn't it? Although I can assure you that's the truth. It's partly because you were so—er—eager to get me home that we had that crash.'

A dull flush warmed his skin. 'You're trying to tell me that accident was my fault?'

'Partly, yes... If you'd been concentrating, we might have had more of a chance.'

'That's not written up in the police report!' he snapped.

'No, I don't suppose it is... A wife is hardly likely to betray her husband, is she? Particularly when she has only been his wife a matter of hours! That report was made with my testimony, don't forget.'

Once more there was an unreadable expression on his face. 'It seems I owe you thanks...'

Jane shrugged. 'You needn't feel too guilty. If the farmer had looked before pulling out into that lane; if he hadn't had too much cider at lunchtime... I should look on it as fate. Because if the accident hadn't happened you could have been stuck with me for life. Now, as long as you leave me alone, you've got a good chance of regaining your freedom, haven't you?'

All the bitterness she was feeling welled up into her mouth, leaving her feeling sick and wretched. 'Now, if you don't mind,' she told him sarcastically, 'I'll go and find my room so I can unpack and rest!'

'Aren't you forgetting something?' he said. Startled, she turned to look back at him. 'Because

you are my wife, Carmen will already have done
your unpacking, and your room is mine . . .'

'Miguel, don't try to play games with me, please.
I've had enough. Now call Carmen and give her
instructions to prepare another room for me, because I don't want my future jeopardised, even if
you don't seem to care!' she snapped.

There was just a moment of bright speculation
in his eyes before he swung away from her. 'Tell
her yourself, Señora Miguel de Tarrago!'

'I'll go and do just that right now!' Jane shouted,
then, turning her back on him, ran away, praying
that the mask of tears that blurred her vision
wouldn't allow her to slip and fall in front of him.

Carmen was far too well trained a servant to show
any surprise at Jane's request, but Jane still felt
guilty all the same. Miguel surely hadn't expected
her to share his bed, had he? To start with, she
found that idea incredible, until she remembered
more clearly that arrogant macho man she'd
married. Of course he'd expected her to sleep with
him. She was the stupid one! It seemed that he'd
decided to accept her, in spite of his cynical words
earlier, but she had too much pride to be taken on
those terms, hadn't she? She rolled over on to the
bed, face down, and beat the mattress hard with
both hands. Hell! She didn't know what she
wanted.

And so began one of the strangest times of her life.
The island, normally so full of tourists, was un-
believably quieter and cooler, and it seemed to Jane
to change its character. Now its long-suffering re-

sidents were to be seen, outnumbering the summer visitors for a change. Everything was the same, yet different, and it was the same between her and Miguel.

He showed no disposition to change her mind over her sleeping arrangements, yet he refused to take any action to annul their marriage, which she found quite extraordinary.

'Miguel!' she attacked him after her first couple of days. 'We must call in the Church. I don't know who to approach. Do you?'

'This wish to end our marriage comes from you!' he told her. 'It has nothing to do with me.'

'But—but... Don't be silly! You told me, that first afternoon, that marriage was the last thing on your mind!' she shouted at him.

'We are married in the sight of God, and I for one am not prepared to take my vows so lightly. How that happened is no longer relevant as far as I am concerned, but I accept the fact that we are now man and wife.'

'How very generous of you!' she answered sarcastically. 'My wishes, of course, don't come into your calculations?'

'I think you are being over-dramatic. You agreed not so very long ago to be my wife. If it weren't for the accident we would by now be lovers, and I don't think you would have been making many complaints.'

'Oh, don't you?' Jane, furious, was on her feet. 'Well, lover-boy,' she spat, 'try remembering that I've been refusing your advances since I was sixteen!

What makes you so sure that we have anything but a marriage of convenience?'

It was Miguel's turn to look totally shocked. 'But no! Never would I have agreed to anything so foolish. Anyway, you accused me of helping to cause the accident by my wish to take you to bed...'

She laughed. 'You sound so sure of yourself, but you're not, are you? You don't know what we agreed, and it looks to me as if you never will!'

Just for a moment Miguel shaded his eyes with one hand, a gesture of such helplessness that just for a moment her heart turned over with love and compassion. What good am I doing? she asked herself. Maybe I should just give in to him—but she hardened her heart as she heard his next words.

'What are your terms for staying with me?' he asked her quietly. 'Are they the same as the ones that made us marry in a church?'

At that exact moment Jane knew that fate had given her a trump card of such power and value that she was half frightened to use it. She forced herself to meet his eyes, her own fiercely candid, yet showing her vulnerability. She clutched her hands behind her back, like a small girl, and stood up straight. 'You promised to love me!' she told him fiercely, daring him to laugh, to deny it, knowing that if he did either of those things it would be the end of everything between them.

'And you think I cheated you...' he told her, his eyes once more alive as they probed hers.

'I know you did!' she accused him bitterly. 'I had my doubts before we married, but everything that's happened since has confirmed it! Why, you even admitted as much when I first arrived out here,' she asserted. 'You as good as admitted that you don't even believe in love!'

Miguel moved quickly, pulling her close to him. 'And how am I to convince you that I only said that because you came flat out with a demand that we annul our marriage?'

Jane fought herself free from his embrace. 'I don't believe you! For some reason you've decided you want our marriage to continue—well——' here she choked on a sob '—I know now that that's impossible...'

'Impossible? No, not now I've found out what the problem is. You lied to me just now, Jane, when you told me I'd promised to love you, didn't you? You saw an opportunity to take advantage of my lack of memory, but it won't work. You have the most transparently honest face I've ever known, and you can't tell a lie—you never could! That's what you wanted me to say, because in your heart of hearts you love me, whether you acknowledge it or not. That's why you married me, and that's why you insisted it should be in a church—because nothing else would have felt right, would it, my darling?'

He took her tenderly into his arms again. 'No, don't fight me, sweetheart! Let me tell you something. Something I should have had the courage to tell you before, but I was afraid...'

'You, afraid?' Her big grey eyes looked up at him, and half filled with tears. 'No, you'd never

be afraid of anything!' she told him fiercely,
fighting to retain her cool.

'Oh, but I was! Frightened of you rejecting me
if I told you how much I loved you; that I had done
for years and years while I waited for you to grow
up.'

Her face was full of open disbelief. 'No! You
only married me because of Patricia...'

'She was a convenient excuse, yes!' Miguel smiled
at her.

'You blackmailed me into agreeing to be your
wife!' she accused him fiercely.

'So I did! I was desperate, you see. Once I'd seen
you again on the island I knew I had to have you
soon.' His arms tightened around her. 'I couldn't
take any more chances with you. I had to be certain
that you would be mine!'

'Why didn't you tell me?' she wailed, beating her
small hands on his chest, until he covered them
gently with his own.

'Hush, my darling! I was afraid...afraid that I
could only make you want me physically. You used
to get so very cross with me, I didn't think you'd
ever be able to really love me... All those times
I'd look into your eyes, but I never saw love. If I
couldn't impress an impressionable little seventeen-
year-old, how could I hope to win you now? Maybe
you were the one girl who'd stay immune to me...'

'Oh, Miguel, what a lot of time you've wasted!
I would never have thought of you being so silly!'

His arms tightened painfully around her. 'I think
something must have gone badly wrong between us

before we got married, because it's obvious from
your body language on the video that you have
grave doubts about me!' he said.

'I was afraid too, you see ...' she whispered. 'I
loved you so much, yet you never once even mentioned love to me. The whole thing was a deal to
save you from Patricia as far as I was concerned.
I had terrible doubts about whether I was doing the
right thing, but I couldn't seem to help myself. I
told myself that if I married you without your love
it would be better than anyone else doing so, because at least I wasn't after your money!'

He found her mouth then, greedily, and she clung
to him tightly before the magic between them melted
her into a passionate, quiescent being so sensitive
to his touch that her skin burned where he caressed
her, and she ached to feel his body against hers, to
be rid of the constriction of clothes, for there to be
no more barriers between them.

'Oh, God!' Miguel's voice, deep and husky, the
tremors of his body, left her in no doubt of her
power over him. She loved him so much. 'You don't
know how much I want you ...' he continued.

'Show me!' Jane whispered against his mouth as
he carried her up to his room. Once there, he released her in the shuttered cool, and her grey eyes
were brilliant as she waited for him to start making
love to her. His enormous bed, its white cover
striped with shadows, exerted an erotic pull. Slowly
she started to undo the tiny buttons that fastened
her top, her fingers made clumsy by desire, until
she managed to shake it off.

Miguel drew a quick deep breath as he saw her breasts straining provocatively against the silk and lace. He moved quickly towards her, one palm caressing the aroused thrust of her nipples, before expertly removing the bra, and bending his head to take one heated tip in his mouth.

Her head fell back in pleasure as heat seemed to explode through her body at his touch. She felt his hands seeking, then removing her skirt, until she was naked apart from her silk panties. His hands slid inside to stroke her bottom, before he suddenly pulled her hard against him, the contact sudden and erotic in the extreme. He gave a groan of pleasure as her body flooded with love.

Impatiently, she tried to undress him, to feel his skin burn against hers as he removed the last of her barriers. He helped, fired by the same hungry impetuosity, until they fell naked together on the bed.

Quivers of sensation ran through her, like ripples on the water, as he started to kiss and explore her body with a delicate but sure touch. His physical arousal she found intensely exciting as tentatively she too explored his body intimately. Desire burned deep in his dark eyes, and his body was tensed as she continued her exploration.

'Dear God!' He caught and held her two hands.

'Don't you like me touching you?' Her eyes pleaded with him, as once more he groaned.

'My darling! You are a virgin. It is for me to try to make this as pleasurable as possible for you, but if you continue to touch me—ah, then I shall not be able to wait, and I may hurt you!'

Her fingers had stilled for a moment, then continued their exploration. She had an emptiness inside, an aching void that needed to be filled by him. A thick inarticulate sound warned her that she'd gone too far. 'I've dreamed of you making love to me for years. I can't wait any longer, Miguel!' she whispered, as she felt his burning hands part her thighs, then she shuddered with pleasure as his fingers found the source of her delight. He entered her with an urgency that seemed to match her own aching need for fulfilment. Her first sharp cry was just a prelude to the rippling delight of the thrusts of his body against her own. He sought and found her mouth, drugging her senses with his kisses, until he found his release deep within her.

Later he lay on one side and watched her, a lazy smile just curving his lips. 'Don't be too disappointed, my darling! The next time it will be better, I promise.'

Her eyes laughed at him. 'But I wasn't disappointed. I'm just sad that we've wasted all these years.'

'We'll make up for them,' he told her.

'Yes...' She snuggled up close to him. 'I hope we won't have to wait too long?'

Miguel ran one of his fingers lightly down her spine, so that she wriggled in delight. 'No, you won't have to wait long, my darling...' And what she read in his dark eyes had her tummy tightening in passionate anticipation.

'Oh, Miguel, I do love you!' she sighed.

'And I you. Let me show you...'

Next Month's Romances

Each month you can choose from a wide variety of romance with Mills & Boon. Below are the new titles to look out for next month, why not ask either Mills & Boon Reader Service or your Newsagent to reserve you a copy of the titles you want to buy — just tick the titles you would like and either post to Reader Service or take it to any Newsagent and ask them to order your books.

Please save me the following titles:	Please tick	√
BREAKING POINT	Emma Darcy	
SUCH DARK MAGIC	Robyn Donald	
AFTER THE BALL	Catherine George	
TWO-TIMING MAN	Roberta Leigh	
HOST OF RICHES	Elizabeth Power	
MASK OF DECEPTION	Sara Wood	
A SOLITARY HEART	Amanda Carpenter	
AFTER THE FIRE	Kay Gregory	
BITTERSWEET YESTERDAYS	Kate Proctor	
YESTERDAY'S PASSION	Catherine O'Connor	
NIGHT OF THE SCORPION	Rosemary Carter	
NO ESCAPING LOVE	Sharon Kendrick	
OUTBACK LEGACY	Elizabeth Duke	
RANSACKED HEART	Jayne Bauling	
STORMY REUNION	Sandra K. Rhoades	
A POINT OF PRIDE	Liz Fielding	

If you would like to order these books in addition to your regular subscription from Mills & Boon Reader Service please send £1.70 per title to: Mills & Boon Reader Service, P.O. Box 236, Croydon, Surrey, CR9 3RU, quote your Subscriber No:...
(If applicable) and complete the name and address details below. Alternatively, these books are available from many local Newsagents including W.H.Smith, J.Menzies, Martins and other paperback stockists from 12th March 1993.

Name:..

Address:..

....Post Code:...........................

To Retailer: If you would like to stock M&B books please contact your regular book/magazine wholesaler for details.

You may be mailed with offers from other reputable companies as a result of this application.
If you would rather not take advantage of these opportunities please tick box ☐

Another Face . . .
Another Identity . . .
Another Chance . . .

When her teenage love turns to hate, Geraldine Frances vows to even the score. After arranging her own "death", she embarks on a dramatic transformation emerging as *Silver*, a hauntingly beautiful and mysterious woman few men would be able to resist.

With a new face and a new identity, she is now ready to destroy the man responsible for her tragic past.

Silver – a life ruled by one all-consuming passion, is Penny Jordan at her very best.

W●RLDWIDE

4 FREE

Romances and 2 FREE gifts just for you!

*You can enjoy all the
heartwarming emotion of true love for FREE!
Discover the heartbreak and the happiness, the emotion and
the tenderness of the modern relationships in
Mills & Boon Romances.*

*We'll send you 4 captivating Romances as a special offer from
Mills & Boon Reader Service, along with the chance to have
6 Romances delivered to your door each month.*

Claim your FREE books and gifts overleaf...

An irresistible offer from Mills & Boon

Here's a personal invitation from Mills & Boon Reader Service, to become a regular reader of Romances. To welcome you, we'd like you to have 4 books, a CUDDLY TEDDY and a special MYSTERY GIFT absolutely FREE.

Then you could look forward each month to receiving 6 brand new Romances, delivered to your door, postage and packing free! Plus our free Newsletter featuring author news, competitions, special offers and much more.

This invitation comes with no strings attached. You may cancel or suspend your subscription at any time, and still keep your free books and gifts.

It's so easy. Send no money now. Simply fill in the coupon below and post it to -
Reader Service, FREEPOST, PO Box 236, Croydon, Surrey CR9 9EL.

NO STAMP REQUIRED

Free Books Coupon

Yes! Please rush me 4 free Romances and 2 free gifts! Please also reserve me a Reader Service subscription. If I decide to subscribe I can look forward to receiving 6 brand new Romances each month for just £10.20, postage and packing free! If I choose not to subscribe I shall write to you within 10 days - I can keep the books and gifts whatever I decide. I may cancel or suspend my subscription at any time. I am over 18 years of age.

Ms/Mrs/Miss/Mr_____ EP31R

Address_____

_____

Postcode_____Signature_____

Offer expires 31st May 1993. The right is reserved to refuse an application and change the terms of this offer. Readers overseas and in Eire please send for details. Southern Africa write to Book Services International Ltd, P.O. Box 42654, Craighall, Transvaal 2024. You may be mailed with offers from other reputable companies as a result of this application.
If you would prefer not to share in this opportunity, please tick box ☐